The Witches

of

Moonlight Ridge

a novel

Ramey Channell

St. Leonard's Field

Birmingham · Atlanta

Author's Note

This book is a work of fiction. Names, characters, places, and incidents are used fictitiously, and any resemblance to actual persons, living or dead, and actual events is purely coincidental.

Citations:
p. 22-23 — A Virgin Just Nineteen Years Old — traditional folk song
p. 28 — Uncle Joe — traditional children's song
p. 81-83 — The Highwayman — (abridged) Alfred Noyes, 1906
p. 95 — In the Pines, also known as Black Girl — traditional American folk song
p. 139-140 — Jacob's Ladder — traditional African American spiritual, 1750 or 1825
p. 145 — "The wayward sisters . . ." — *Macbeth*, Act I, Scene 3, by William Shakespeare (1564-1616)
p. 165-166 — All Things Bright and Beautiful — Cecil Frances Alexander, 1848

"*The Witches of Moonlight Ridge* is storytelling at its very best. Ramey Channell has a voice that rings true -- lyrical, compelling, and southern."
— Vicki Marsh Covington, author, *The Last Hotel for Women*

"A pure delight by a gifted storyteller! I couldn't put down these tales of growing up on Moonlight Ridge, and found myself smiling until it hurt. Ramey Channell applies her poet's ear for language to stories of a time and place long gone but preserved in memories laced with fantasy and joy. This book is the antidote for the evening news blues."
— Barry Marks, author, *Dividing by Zero*

"Ramey Channell is a Southern writer with the chops of Harper Lee and the sometimes bawdy humor of Mark Twain. In *The Witches of Moonlight Ridge*, Willie T. and Lily Claire are back, and as delightful as ever. You'll laugh, you'll cry, but most of all, you'll be completely charmed."
— Smoky Zeidel, author, *The Storyteller's Bracelet*, and *The Cabin*

For my sisters, Joanne and Susan.

Acknowledgements

Thanks to the following people who read early drafts of portions of this story and gave encouragement, support, and graciously cheered me on: Joanne Cage, Susan Cleveland, Joan Dawson, and Buffy Hosey. Thanks to Ellen Davis, Carole Miller, and Nell Richardson for their encouragement. Thanks to the Open Circle Poetry Group. Thanks to the staff and patrons of Leeds Jane Culbreth Library.

Special thanks to Vicki Marsh Covington, Barry Marks, and Smoky Zeidel.

Thanks to Buffy Hosey for proofreading and editing support.

Thanks to India Dyer for being good with the technology.

Thanks to Jed Cage for his technological help and expertise.

And as always, thanks to my cousin, Donnie Lee Nock, for enduring friendship and never-ending inspiration.

"The true mystery of the world is the visible, not the invisible."

— *Oscar Wilde*

Prologue

My cousin, Willie T., and I were born on the same day, in the same hospital room, and folks say we looked so much alike we could have been twins. My mama, Sara Nash, and my Aunt Rachel Nock got into a fight with each other while giving birth, and Dr. Carlisle, who delivered me, accused my mama of having no maternal instincts whatsoever. Dr. Driggers, who was drunk at the time, delivered my cousin because Dr. Carlisle wasn't able to handle both crazy women at the same time.

After my cousin and I were born, while everybody was in the process of recovering from the ordeal, my daddy, Sam Nash, brought my mama a sweet bouquet of lilies of the valley, and so they named me Lily Claire Carlisle Nash. My Uncle Buddy Nock brought Aunt Rachel a bunch of yellow stink weeds that he pulled on the side of the road, and so they named my cousin after our Great-Granddaddy, William Theophilus Greenberry, a renowned crazy man who loved bugs and possums.

William Theophilus Greenberry Nock, Willie T., was not just my cousin; he was also my best friend. We lived on a mountain called Moonlight Ridge, just outside of a little town named Eden, Alabama, at a time when we were able to roam the woods in search of playtime, adventure, and magic, with just about as much freedom as two carefree hound pups. Our parents and grandparents considered us to be wise enough to take care of ourselves, and about the only firm rules were "Don't kill each other," and "Be home before dark." And even the "Be home before dark," wasn't always firmly enforced.

Seasons on the mountain came and went, and Willie T. and I learned to accept the mysteries and magic around us with very few questions. As far as we were concerned, fascinating people, frightful creatures, and fantastic events were all just part of life, out on the mountain.

One

A Man of Letters

The story I have to tell is probably just about the strangest and most amazing tale you'd ever want to hear. When I was a child up on the mountain, the world we inhabited was like living with one foot in reality and one foot in a make-believe dream all the time. Old family stories, told over and over again, along with the most astonishing and hair-raising sights anybody could imagine, turned day-to-day life into a constant and puzzling adventure.

Summer was mostly a fun time; days were long and nights were eerily quiet, but calm and peaceful. But, every single year when autumn rolled around, as my granddaddy used to say, there was no telling which way the cat would jump. I think what he meant was that there's just no way to guess what's likely to happen out on the mountain at that time of the year. With autumn days getting shorter, leaves fell in a rustling golden shower onto the cool damp ground, and trees began to look like gnarled and twisted old witches against an unpredictable sky. Owls stayed close to the house, hooting and screeching all night long, and in the daytime entire flocks of peevish black crows roamed around the yards and fields. They walked around on their stiff little legs like black, beady-eyed little men, communicating with one another in some mysterious crow-language, while keeping watch over everything that happened day-in and day-out. A crow is just about the nosiest creature in the whole creation. Nothing in the world makes a crow happier than sticking his nose in somebody else's business, but they're familiar and mostly good-natured, which is more than you could say about some of the things that roamed around Moonlight Ridge.

That fall when my cousin, Willie T. Nock, and I entered the fourth grade, the excitement of starting a new school year purely overtook us, and about the only thing we were thinking about was learning the ups and downs of a new teacher. Both of us ended up in Miss Tomkins' room, and we couldn't have been any happier if somebody had told us we were going to spend the next nine months in a room with the Good Fairy herself. Miss Tomkins was a jolly, rather plump, white haired woman who had been teaching at Eden Elementary School so long that my mother, Sara Nash, and my aunt, Rachel Nock, had been in her room way back when they were both in the fourth grade. My mother's mama, Granny Rilla, purely adored Winnie Lee Tomkins, and my grandparents on my daddy's side, Mawmaw Annie Laurie and Papa Jasper Nash, considered her to be some style of aristocracy come to earth in Eden, Alabama.

But, disaster struck. One week after Miss Winnie Lee Tomkins welcomed us to her fourth grade class, with all of us feeling like big shots because we knew we had the best teacher in the whole wide world, the esteemed and beloved lady stepped on a hickory nut on her back porch, lost her balance, and fell down her back steps, breaking her right wrist and her sizeable right hip.

On Monday morning of the second week of school, all us joyfully expectant Tomkins students were met by the alarming sight of the gaunt and bony elementary school principal, Mr. Vales, who was good natured and likeable enough but, I swear, looked just like a beady-eyed black crow. His nose was long and sharp looking like a beak, and his hair was black and oiled to a slick shine over his head. His eyebrows sprouted out like black pin-feathers over his bright little coal-black eyes. He waited ominously in front of the blackboard in Miss Tomkins' classroom until we were all seated and pretty much at his mercy. Then he made the sad announcement that our Good Fairy teacher's hip, a word we all thought you weren't supposed to say, was broke all to hell and back, which we knew you weren't supposed to say, and she would have to be replaced by some other teacher, whose actual identity was as yet unknown and a total mystery.

The resulting wail that broke out instantly and simultaneously from every individual student upon hearing this report was enough to fill the entire classroom with a deafening cacophony which in turn caused Old Crow Face a near-about heart attack. He flapped his arms up in the air a few times, a look of shock and remorse on his haggard face that did nothing to comfort or reassure all of us bawling fourth-graders, then fled the room with both hands on the top of his oily head. Within seconds he returned, dragging with him an unsuspecting passer-by who had just dropped off his little brother in the room across the hall. That unfortunate fellow happened to be Erskine Batson, the thin-as-a-rail, just-turned twenty year old driver of the garbage truck that made the rounds every Saturday morning throughout the highways and the by-ways of Eden, picking up soggy paper sacks stuffed with reeking household trash and emptying the dented, World War II era garbage cans.

As it turned out, Erskine was not only real handy at picking up trash and hauling it off to the garbage dump; he was also the brother-in-law of one of our neighbors, Cowboy Howard, and he had attended college in Kentucky for one year. His sister, Estaleen, married to Cowboy Howard, hadn't even finished high school, but somewhere in the unknown world was a well-to-do relative who'd tried sending Erskine off to get a college education.

The way the story goes, Erskine cried the day they put him on the train to Kentucky, called everybody within earshot all manner of horrible names, and yelled "God damn a college!" Then he hauled off and kicked one of the colored porters who hadn't done a thing in the world to him as the train pulled away from the Eden train depot. Nobody expected the disgruntled, overall clad, barefoot country boy to remain in Kentucky long enough to become educated, if indeed he even stayed on the train all the way to the far away college. But, he stayed a'way up there for one entire year. Then he got the measles and came home to Batson Holler on the off side of Moonlight Ridge, the pride of his mama and daddy and all his kinfolks. As far as they were concerned, one year of college was enough, and as far as Erskine was concerned, it was just about one year too much.

So, with one year of college under his belt, the mystifying habit of walking around in the woods cussing and reciting poetry, and every day free to do as he pleased, except Saturdays when he drove the worse-for-wear Eden garbage truck, Erskine Batson looked like an apt replacement for our tragically stove-up Good Fairy teacher.

"Why don't y'all quit cryin' now?" Mr. Vales urged us in his nasally whine as he hauled the unenlightened Erskine Batson to the front of the room and positioned the tall, undernourished young man in front of the blackboard.

"Look who's come to our rescue, if he'll agree to help us out? It's like a miracle! And Miss Tomkins'll be so proud to know her pupils are well taken care of. And by a man of letters!"

Erskine displayed a baffled grin, ducked his head a little and looked up from under his eyebrows at Mr. Vales. He snorted and rubbed his knuckles against his nose as he eyed Old Crow Face, who at this point was standing with arms outstretched, like he was offering us a pure-dee treasure.

After a few moments of silence, during which all the fourth-graders had ceased crying and were attentively eye-balling the two men in front of us, Erskine Batson leaned toward the principal and whispered, "Are you offerin' me a

6

teachin' job here, 'Fessor Vales?"

Mr. Vales' relief was immediately apparent.

"See there?" he announced, gesturing once again in Erskine's direction and gazing out at the roomful of bemused students. "We'll all be fine, won't we? And won't Miss Tomkins be proud? She was so greatly concerned for the welfare of her little pupils. So greatly concerned, with her hip and all."

And with that, Mr. Vales and Erskine shook hands and Mr. Vales fell to slapping Erskine on the back with surprising zeal; then he turned on his heel, escaped out into the hallway and disappeared with amazing speed.

So, that's how me and Willie T. ended up being taught more than we ever intended to learn about long division, decimals, fractions, square roots, iambic pentameter, music theory, and the ins and outs of garbage collection, from Erskine Batson, who could easily have been deemed "Most unlikely to be a fourth grade teacher."

Like so many teachers, Erskine proved to be a great one for talking, and as he settled in to his appointed position as Substitute Good Fairy Teacher, he veered off onto many strange and varied subjects, sometimes to the delight of the fourth graders in his classroom, and sometimes to our absolute and total puzzlement. He took to quoting William Shakespeare morning, noon, and night, read poetry that sometimes made us laugh and sometimes made us cry, told us that Napoleon wasn't actually in Waterloo, Belgium, when he met his Waterloo, and informed us that we were all citizens of The Solar System, with planets circling the sun and not the other way around. Rummaging through the cloak room, he found some sort of mysterious triangular wooden contraption with a piece of chalk on one end, and used it to magically produce a series of perfectly round circles on the dusty, chipped blackboard, then informed us that this was the alignment of all the planets circling the huge round sun right in the middle.

After labeling all the planets with their proper names, Erskine stood back for about a minute and silently studied the blackboard and his impressive rendering of our solar system. Then he changed subjects. We all soon learned that Erskine Batson was inclined to jump from subject to subject like a grasshopper on a hot stove.

"Now, if you'll all learn to exercise your eyeballs," he announced to the class, "won't a one of you ever have to wear eye-glasses, thereby saving yourselves and your loved ones a world of expense and grief as the years roll by."

Toward that end, he had us all to sit with our yellow #2 pencils right in front of our noses, then directed us to shift our gaze back and forth from the yellow pencil to one of the planets in his illustration of the solar system on the blackboard.

"Pencil, Pluto! Pencil, Pluto!" Erskine called out, over and over, till we were all plumb wore out with our exercised eyeballs. Twice a day, morning and afternoon, it was "Pencil, Pluto! Pencil, Pluto!" with all us fourth graders dutifully chanting along and cutting our eyes this way and that. It wasn't long before the whole solar system had been erased from the blackboard for one reason or another, and in its place, much to our surprise and amusement, Erskine drew a pretty fair likeness of the cartoon character, Pluto the Dog. And when the delegation of certified optometrists from Birmingham came out to test everybody's eyes to see who needed glasses, the doctor declared he'd never in his life seen younguns with such good eyesight and strong eyeballs as we all had in Erskine Batson's room.

Being a dyed-in-the-wool music lover, as all Batsons are, Erskine also did a tolerable job of teaching us what he called music theory. He told us that every note has a letter name, A, B, C, D, E, F, or G; but it stops at G and then starts all over again at A. He rambled on about whole notes and half notes and quarter notes, and to illustrate this he drew pictures of whole apples and half apples and quarter apples on the blackboard, which made us all want to eat an apple. Then he launched into the mysteries of some dead fellow named Pythagorus, who, before he died, came up with a whole mess of ideas about notes and tones and perfect intervals and number intervals. Erskine insisted it was as simple as pie. And come to think of it, he said, pie also had a number which he told us was 3.14 and some odd. But it wasn't near as simple as he said, and the tidbit about the pie muddied the waters something awful and made us all wish we had an apple pie.

Finally, we all pretty much got the hang of it after he had to confess that pie was another subject entirely and didn't actually have anything to do with the subject of music intervals, and he explained that an interval was the number of letter names from one note to another. And we all ended up feeling like musical geniuses when he drew the white keys and the black keys of a piano on the blackboard, and had us all come up and practice counting eighths and fifths and fourths and so on. Then he told us there were all sorts of songs you could use to memorize what all the intervals sounded like. He demonstrated how the first two notes of "Somewhere Over the Rainbow" is an eighth, the first twinkle and the second twinkle in "Twinkle, Twinkle Little Star" is a fifth, the first two notes of "Here Comes the Bride" is a fourth, and the first two notes of "Happy Birthday" is just a plain old one.

We had a genuine for-real music teacher from the county board of education, a delicate looking young woman named Miss Puck, who came to Eden Elementary once a week to teach us how to sing fancy high-brow songs. And when we informed her of all the musical revelations we had learned from Erskine Batson, she gazed upon our skinny hill-billy teacher like he was Mr. W.A. Mozart in the flesh! The dreamy look that came over Miss Puck's face every time she cast her eyes in Erskine Batson's direction was a sight to behold. It just goes to show you. The love of music can do strange things to the human brain.

But of all the strange and peculiar subjects he introduced us to, what Erskine liked to talk about the most, the thing we learned from him that would end up changing our lives and his, was his favorite subject from that far-away college. Erskine Batson brought back with him a love and obsession of digging up old stuff from the past, things that were probably better off not dug up to begin with, forgotten mysteries that might have been better off forgotten. And he called this the Science of Archaeology.

My cousin and I were immediately overcome by the archaeology bug. We spent hours listening to stories about the amazing stuff archaeologists found when they dug around in Egypt, and the mysteries of the Aztecs in Mexico, and the long-ago people who had lived right here in Alabama and all over the world. Erskine convinced us that there was nothing in the whole world more tantalizing than digging in the dirt and finding things he called artifacts, lost and buried treasures from the past.

My mama and daddy didn't seem to mind me bringing home muddy lumps of dug up treasure, and they gazed appreciatively at the bits of broken glass, old dirty pennies, buttons, and chipped marbles that Willie T. and I had found on our digging excursions. But when we brought in tiny fragments of bone, strange and sometimes scary looking fossils, and the odd tooth, either human or animal, my granddaddy, Papa Jasper Nash, called it "disturbing the dead," and predicted that we'd all wind up digging up trouble.

Two

Witch Boy

The first days of autumn on Moonlight Ridge felt like a kind of paradise. The mountain and everything on it, including the people, seemed to relax and breathe easy. After the raging heat and humidity of summer subsided just a little, we were left with gentle warm days when the air around us and the sky above us became crystal clear and expansive. Days were fragrant with the spicy scent of leaves changing colors on sweet gum, dogwood, and maple, mixed with the sharp green scent of tall pines and flourishing cedars. Nights were cooler, the mosquitoes had pretty much decided to call it quits, and dreamy sleep beside an open bedroom window was blessed by gentle, friendly breezes.

Inspired by the tales told by our teacher, Willie T. and I spent entire days in the woods searching for treasure and finding it in abundance. Genuine fossils, sharp-edged arrow heads, old pennies worn smooth from handling, and interesting rocks with puzzling shapes were enough to thrill and delight any child who came across them and picked them up.

And, occasionally, there would be something entirely unexpected and puzzling. Things like one ruby earring, crusted with dirt and caked with dried mud; a smooth round ball, just the right size to fit in your hand, perfectly formed of solid rock; a couple of worn silver dollars, marked 1879, melted and stuck together; a brown half-grown dog, lost in the woods and eager to go home with us, bearing a curious little spring stuck on the end of his thin tail.

The way we discovered that the dog had a spring stuck on his tail was that he looked right at me and told me his tail was hurting.

"Leave that mangy ol' dog alone, Lily C.," my cousin insisted. "Let's go home and see if Aunt Sara has any tea in the Frigidaire. My craw is parched."

Willie T. was my best friend, but he was a trial and a tribulation just the same.

"Wait a minute," I told him, looking deep into the dog's intelligent-looking brown eyes. "He's talking to me ... let me see..."

"Talking to you?" Willie T. croaked. "What in the world do you mean? That dog ain't said a dang word."

"He did so," I insisted.

Up to that time, I don't believe I had ever heard an animal say *anything* before, but right then I knew that this funny looking brown dog had spoken to me.

"He said his tail was hurting him," I added. I put both my hands on the dog's lean brown back, trying to turn him so I could inspect his tail.

The dog bared his teeth, wiggled his lips and tried to bite me.

"Gyah!" my cousin yelled. "You're gonna get bit! Don't touch that gall-durn dog!"

"He's just skittish ... 'cause his tail hurts."

Willie T. scowled and snorted.

I patted the dog softly on his knobby head, and ran my hand down his back. He was really a pretty dog, long leggedy and lean, with a nice long muzzle and a big shiny black nose. But that poor old tail was just a'droopin'.

"Here, buddy," I whispered to him. "Let me see. What's

makin' your old tail hurt?"

The dog started whimpering, and twisted around to look at his own tail. He jumped around, snapping the air, trying to grab the end of his tail in his mouth. 'Round and 'round he twirled, chasing his tail and snapping at the air.

Willie T. watched, hands on his hips, leaning toward the dog to get a better look at the animal and its tail.

"Here, dammit," he exclaimed impatiently. "It's makin' me dizzy to watch this!"

And he grabbed the dog around its middle and hoisted the writhing animal up into his arms.

"Get still, you blamed crazy dog," he commanded. "Let us see if it's something wrong with your damned tail or not!"

Willie T. was bad to cuss any time he felt like it.

The dog yelped like he'd been kicked, and looked back and forth, first at the boy holding him, then at me. He gave a big kick and leaped out of Willie T.'s arms, landed on the ground and started spinning around again, trying to catch ahold of his tail. Willie T. fell into the spirit of the chase and started grabbing at the dog as it whirled around.

"Grab him, Lily C.! Get a hold of him! Get him!" he yelled.

Finally, I managed to get my hands on the frantic animal again, and I whispered and crooned, rubbing his head and his long brown spine. "Let us see, buddy," I begged him. "Let us look at your old tail."

Willie T. wrapped one arm around the dog's neck in a death grip.

"Prob'ly the rabies," he muttered disgustedly. "My mama'll kill me if I get the rabies."

I petted the dog's rump, then got ahold of the long tail.

"Look at this! He's got somethin' stuck on his tail," I told Willie T. "It's some kind of a spring!"

"Can you pull it off?" my cousin asked, eyeing the end of the dog's tail as I held it aloft for inspection. It looked horrible, all raw and sore looking, with just a few sparse hairs sticking out of the swollen skin between the spirals of embedded metal wire.

"It's tight as Uncle Dick's hatband," I answered. "It must have been stuck on there for a long time. How in the world do you reckon he got a spring caught on the end of his tail?"

"Pull it," Willie T. instructed. "See if it'll pull off."

To tell the gospel truth, I didn't much feel like handling the afflicted end of the dog's tail. It looked really red and blistery, and pitifully sore. But I didn't know anything else to do. So, holding the momentarily quiet dog's tail in one hand, I just barely touched the curious spring, planning to pull at it to see if I could prize it off.

I couldn't hardly believe my eyes! The instant I touched the metal spring, it popped off the end of the dog's tail and flew through the air like a miniature space ship! The dog gave a loud screech, and pulled away from me and Willie T., then turned around a couple of times, looking at the suddenly liberated tip of his poor old tail.

"What happened?" Willie T. demanded. "Did the end of his tail come plumb off?"

"No, it was the spring!" I answered. "It boinged off his tail and flew through the air..."

Willie T. laughed a funny little nervous laugh. "Gyah! I seen it!" he chuckled. "Ain't that the most peculiar thang! Where'd it go?"

I started searching the dusty ground around our feet, wanting to get a closer look at the mysterious metal coil. Willie T. and I looked all around, prodding the loose dirt and closely inspecting every pebble and gravel. But we couldn't locate the metal spring anywhere. It had flown away.

We finally gave up searching and looked at the brown dog, lying on his back in the gravelly dirt, wiggling back and forth like a maniac. After a minute of cavorting around on his back, he hopped up, shook the dirt off his back, gave me and Willie T. an adoring gaze, then barked a joyful note.

Willie T. and I walked home down the mountain trail,

under orange and gold maples, red dogwoods, and sweet smelling green pines. The autumn wind came down the mountain behind us, pushing at our backs and shaking the tree limbs over our heads. Above the rustling trees, the sky was as blue as a robin's egg.

"I bet you it was a witch put that spring on that dog's tail," Willie T. announced as we walked along the dirt path. "Witches do thangs like that ... and whatever and all."

"Springs on dogs' tails? Why in the world would a witch put a spring on a dog's tail? You're just makin' that up, and you know it." I punched Willie T. just about as hard as I could, and we became embroiled in a brief scuffle. The dog barked at us, crouching down with his long front legs braced out in front of him.

"I'm tellin' you," my cousin insisted, pushing me away from him as we continued on down the dirt road. "I heard Mama and Daddy talkin' about it, just the other night. Said they's witches out here on Moonlight Ridge; have been since time in memorial, Mama said. I bet you a dollar and a half it was a witch put that spring on there. A magic spell or somethin'. It ain't no tellin' what."

I wondered how he ever came up with such a crazy idea, but I couldn't think of any other probable way that a dog could get a metal spring lodged on his tail unless somebody stuck it on there on purpose.

The dog walked with us, all the way home. And that's how we came to have a brown dog named Witch Boy.

Three

Papa and the Loup-Garou

Papa Jasper Nash, my daddy's daddy, loved to tell scary stories about the old days and all manner of peculiar things that had occurred out on the mountain. He had often told us all about the loup-garou, a half-man, half-wolf creature who prowled around on the mountain at night, trying to catch you outside in the dark or while you were asleep in your bed. Papa called him "the rougarou," and said he'd sneak into your house at night while you were sleeping, with his old nasty long hair and long dirty finger nails, and you'd wake up with him leaning over your bed.

"I got you now, me!" he'd growl, then grab you with his long sharp claws. And there's no way to get loose from him once he's got you, Papa said, 'cause a loup-garou can hypnotize you just by looking you in the eye.

That's why Papa told us to always hang the fly-swatter or the tea strainer by the back door at night before you went to bed. Because the loup-garou is real curious, really mean but also sort of dumb and simple-minded, and anything little bitty catches his attention and he can't quit looking at it.

16

When he sees a fly swatter or a tea strainer, all those little bitty holes puzzle him, and he'll stand there all night long, just mesmerized and trying to figure out what all those little bitty holes are there for, and trying to count to see how many there are. So when dawn comes he'll still be standing there outside the back door, staring at the little holes, and when it gets daylight he'll run away and never make it into your house to get you and say "I got you now, me."

Papa Jasper and Mawmaw Annie Laurie were a quaint pair. Papa was half Apache, brown as a tough old acorn, and never at a loss for a scary story to tell. Mawmaw Annie Laurie was a fair-skinned Isbell, her eyes were bright blue and twinkly, and she had the sweetest smile. But she was cantankerous and full of mischief, and she loved a scary story as much as the rest of us did. I guess living out in the deep woods in a place like Moonlight Ridge, it just seemed natural to believe in boogers.

There was nothing in the world my cousin and I liked better than spending the night at Mawmaw and Papa's house. When autumn settled in on the mountain, it got dark early in the evening, and my grandparents' little wooden house sat up in the dark woods, high on top of a ridge all by itself. The way the wind would blow and whistle around the little house, and under the front door, making a long mournful sound like a train whistle; it sure made all Mawmaw and Papa's scary stories sound real, and we'd hunker down in front of the old stone fireplace, listening to the wind on Moonlight Ridge.

I believe, for better or worse, Willie T. inherited his amazing story tellin' skills from listening to all those tales that Mawmaw and Papa told us. But he was hard-put to sit still. When Papa was trying to tell us a story, if Willie T. interrupted right at the worst part of the tale, which he frequently did, Mawmaw always picked up her hickory switch and handed it to me.

"Here, Lily Claire! Will you warp that youngun?"

Then I'd whack him a couple of perfunctory warps before

17

he could grab the switch away from me.

"I'm listenin'!" Willie T. protested. "Uncle Jasper, tell her to quit hittin' me, now. I'm a'listenin' to ever' word!"

"Listen then, and quit that jabberin'. Go ahead, Jasper," Mawmaw instructed, while retrieving the hickory switch from us. "Tell about that time you watched the loup-garou runnin' down the road after the preacher."

"Why, I was just a young man, then," Papa started off, running his hand through his thick white head of hair, then giving his chin a couple of thoughtful scratches. "That new preacher come here from down in Montgomery County, and he didn't know a thing in the world about how to get along up here on the mountain. Wore the silliest mess of clothes you ever saw! Stripe'd pants and a fancy weskit and a bow tie, and a straw hat ever' where he went!

"Well, one evenin' I was comin' home late from the Greenberry place. W.T. Greenberry was always puttin' on one kind of a shindig or another. Jack Levert was always there, playin' that fiddle. If you could get in the front door, why, you could have a good time!"

"W.T. made moonshine didn't he?" Mawmaw interjected. Papa nodded gravely.

"And sweet muscadine wine!" he replied. "Best you ever tasted. Well, I'd tasted a little, and was just headed home in the dark of the night. Then the moon come up, just as big and yeller up over the ridge, and I was strollin' along, singin' that old tune, "She Claimed She Was a Virgin, Just Nineteen Years Old.""

"Sing it, Uncle Jasper!" Willie T. interrupted. "Sing that'n for us!"

"Let him finish the story first," Mawmaw commanded, reaching around me to whack in Willie T.'s general direction with her ever-ready hickory.

"Well, I come around a bend in the road, and yonder come that preacher in the dark, traipsin' along in all of his sissy-lookin' outfit. I left off singin', but he cut his eyes at me

18

and said he'd heard that sinful song comin' out of my mouth, and he'd be ashamed if he's me.

"Just then I heard the awfullest commotion in the bushes, and out jumped the ugliest lookin' haint you've ever seen. Hair all matted and wearin' nothin' but nasty rags of clothes.

" 'Run for your life!' I hollered at that preacher. 'It's the rougarou!' And I took off down the road a piece, just a'tearin' up the trail to get away."

Willie T., by this time, was bouncing up and down like a worm in hot ashes, his sweaty face gleaming in the firelight. "What happened then? What happened then, Uncle Jasper?" he squawked.

My granddaddy continued, leaning toward us as he spoke. "I figured he had us both, for sure. Made the hair stand up on the back of my neck, I was so scared. But I took a quick look back to see if he was gainin' on me, and there stood that fancy preacher, a'diggin' in his vest pocket for his eye-glasses!"

Papa clapped his hands with glee, and he and Mawmaw both laughed out loud. Papa fiddled around at his shirt pocket like he was picking a pair of glasses out, and then he imitated the preacher, fixing the glasses on his nose and hooking the wires behind his ears. Then he cocked his head from side to side in a prissy way, like he was trying to focus his eyes on something in front of him.

" 'You better get from there!' I yelled at the preacher. 'Hit's the rougarou!' But he looked like he was already cast under a spell, just a gazin' at that ugly lookin' booger in front of him. Lookin' right into its eyes! Now, anybody knows better than to do that!

"Well, all of a sudden, the moon come out from behind a cloud, and that preacher got a good look at what it was a'standin' right in his face. And 'Whaaaa-whaaaa?' he bellered, and he took off down the road, just a'gettin' it!

"That's when the rougarou cast his hateful eye over at me. I liked to fainted plumb dead to the world! But he just gave

19

me that one evil glare, then he dropped down on his all-fours, and took out lopin' after that preacher."

"Umm umm," Mawmaw grunted. "The lord a'mercy!"

Willie T. and I looked at each other, and my cousin's eye balls were big around as a hoot owl in the dark.

"I figgered I'd better do somethin' or that thing was gonna eat up the preacher, so I picked up a few rocks and ran a little piece after 'em, pitchin' those rocks as hard as I could. Pinged him a couple a'times, but he never slowed up. Him and the fancy preacher went out of sight through the bushes … and of all the thrashin' and wallerin' and leaves a flyin' out into the road!"

"Why, Jasper? It got him!" Mawmaw breathed.

"Well," Papa continued. "Ever'thing got just as quiet, and I hunkered down in the road to see through the bushes what I could see. And all of a sudden, here come the preacher, tearin' through the brush! Nearly ran right over me, and we got tangled up with one another in the middle of the road. That preacher was white in the face, and he'd lost his eye-glasses and his straw hat somewheres in the thicket! He got a'loose from me and tore out a'runnin' again, yellin', 'Whoooo, lordy! Whoooo, lordy!' And I was about to take off a'runnin' in the other direction, when out come the rougarou, that preacher's straw hat clutched in his dirty fist, and the slobber just a runnin' out of his crooked jaws!"

"And I was plumb froze!" Papa told us.

A dreadful shiver ran down my spine, and Willie T. gasped, gripping the edge of his chair, his mouth hanging open.

"That's the closest I ever come to being scared slap to death. And that ol' rougarou walked right past me, so close I could smell him stinkin'. Never smelled of anything so vile."

We all waited, but it seemed to me like that was all Papa intended to say about it.

"Did you get away from it?" Willie T. asked.

Papa looked at us, with a sort of far-away look on his

face, and I knew he was remembering how he felt, standing that close to the nasty scary loup-garou.

"He was hypnotized by that straw hat," Papa marveled. "All them little holes in the straw hat saved me. The preacher, too. We both got clean away..."

"Lord-a-mercy!" Willie T. exclaimed. "Don't talk about it no more! A possum has done run over my grave!"

"You're scarin' the younguns, Jasper," Mawmaw cautioned.

Just then a big gust of wind blew the front door open with a loud bang, and we all nearly jumped into the fireplace! Witch Boy jumped up from the floor where he'd been sound asleep, and started barking up a storm. Mawmaw hopped up so fast, she knocked her chair over, and it fell on top of the dog and made him yelp and bark even louder. Willie T. grabbed ahold of me and tried to drag me with him away from the gaping front door. Outside the wind was howling through the dark woods.

"Now, look," Mawmaw complained. "You've scared us good."

Papa picked up the fallen chair.

"Turn her a'loose, William," he said as he prized Willie T.'s fingers off my arms. "It's all the truth. Jack Levert always said he thought that rougarou had followed his folks up here from down in the bayou. And, man alive, he was afraid of that thing!

"Hush, dog!" he scolded Witch Boy. The dog hushed up his barking and looked apologetic. "My folks come from down that way, too. They were all down there at Fort Searcy, near Mobile, with the Old Man before he was sent out to Oklahoma. And my mama used to scare the daylights out of us, talkin' about the rougarou."

Papa walked over to the open front door and cautiously poked his head out, taking a quick glance into the dark yard, then closed the door, shutting out the night wind.

"Y'all set back down," he said, picking up his old guitar

from out of a dark corner of the room. "And I'll sing you that song if I can remember it all. You remember it don't you, Laurie?"

Mawmaw clucked and hummed as we all sat back down, our nerves a little jangled but no worse for wear.

Papa sat down and strummed the guitar a few times, twisted a couple of tuning pegs, and plucked a string or two. Witch Boy, magically soothed by the sounds of the guitar, turned around and around, then curled up at Papa's feet.

And then, in the darkened little house in the middle of the scary dark night, Papa Jasper sang a ridiculous and somewhat unsettling song.

A Virgin, Just Nineteen Years Old

As I was out walking one night by the strand
I met a young damsel all dressed up so grand
She was dressed all so fine, with jewels of gold
And she said she was a virgin, just nineteen years old

Her fingers were tapered, her neck like a swan
Her lips were like rubies, her voice not too strong
In three weeks we were married, and the wedding bells tolled
I had married a virgin, just nineteen years old

The wedding party broke up, we retired to rest
But my hair stood upright when my bride she undressed
For a cart-load of padding my young bride did unfold
And she claimed she was a virgin. just nineteen years old

First she took off her slippers, about a foot wide
Then she took off her left ear and laid it aside
When out on the carpet her glass eye did roll
And she claimed she was a virgin, just nineteen years old

Next she unscrewed her left leg as far as the knee
Then pulled off her fingers, I counted just three
Then on her left shoulder, a large hump I did behold
And she claimed to be a virgin only nineteen years old

When she wiped off her eyebrows I thought I should faint
And she scraped from her thin cheeks a cart-load of paint
She pulled off her black wig, then her bald head soon told
That she was an old virgin, more than nineteen years old

When she pulled out her false teeth, I jumped up in terror
For her nose and her chin very near stuck together
From the chamber I ran, never more to behold
The virgin not nineteen, but ninety-nine years old

Now, come all you young fellows when a'courting you go
Examine your true love from her head to her toe
For if you don't do it, you're bound to be sold
To a patched up old maid, about ninety years old

By the time Papa finished the song, Mawmaw was laughing and wiping her eyes.

"I don't believe that song's fit to be sung in front of these younguns," she chuckled. "Lord, Willie T., don't breathe a word of it around Rachel!"

We all laughed at that. My Aunt Rachel, Willie T.'s mama, didn't have a funny bone in her entire body. She hardly ever cracked a smile, pretty much dedicated her entire existence to working crossword puzzles, and had give up trying to solve Willie T. a long time ago.

Papa put his guitar back in the corner, then grabbed the heavy iron poker and stirred up the fire, causing bright orange flames to leap and dance in the fireplace.

"Y'all get you an extra quilt over there," Papa warned.

"Farmer's Almanac says it's 'spose to be a cold one tonight. I expect when we get up in the mornin', it'll be frost on the punkin'."

That night, me and Willie T. and Witch Boy slept on a pallet on the floor, right up as close as we could get to Mawmaw and Papa's bed. The drowsy fire crackled and popped in the fireplace beside us, and the wind howled and moaned out in the woods, like some dark prowling animal, all night long.

When we woke up the next morning, sure enough, it was frost on the punkin'!

Four

Indian Summer

Waking up on a clear frosty morning at my grandparents' house was an invigorating experience. The ashes in the fireplace had gone cold, so me and Willie T. both wrapped ourselves up in quilts and hustled into the kitchen to hover near the warm stove. Sun peeked through Mawmaw's ancient, threadbare, calico curtains on the little kitchen window, scattering sunlight designs across the stained and pock-marked oilcloth on the kitchen table. A small cut-glass bowl of amber honey sat alone in the middle of the table, and a pan of biscuits along with a pot of Mawmaw's inevitable oatmeal was still warm on the wood-fired stove. A near-deafening, clanging noise issued from the back yard.

"Callin' them bees," Willie T. muttered as he plopped a big blob of oats into a blue pottery bowl, grabbed a biscuit, and sat wrapped in his quilt at the sunny table.

Through the window I could see her, standing out beside the little back porch, whacking a large spoon against the bottom of an empty, beat-up aluminum pan just as hard as she could.

"Heeeere, bees. Heeeere, bees," she called, just the way most people call pigs. "Come on bees. Heeeere bees."

She stopped abruptly, stomped up the wooden steps, and flung open the back door, letting in a gust of cold early morning air.

Willie T. looked up from his oatmeal bowl and grumbled, "Personal, I don't believe bees have ears."

"Ears? The lord a'mercy!" Mawmaw exclaimed. "What in the world are you talkin' about now? Mornin' Lily Claire."

"Why are you makin' that awful noise, if the bees cain't hear it anyways?" Willie T. asked around a mouthful of oatmeal. I was pretty interested in hearing the answer to that question myself.

"That's the way I call my bees back to the hive. They'll all leave the hive and go flying off someplace; you can see 'em out there, up in a tree. Then I have to witch 'em back. I beat on that pan to make them swarm, then when they get ready, they all come back to the hive. Jasper's mama taught me how to call a swarm of bees. Apache. That's how I've always done it." Mawmaw tossed the empty pan into the bottom of the cupboard. "Ears! They're bees, they don't have to have ears. But they can hear just as good as anybody."

I carried my pink bowl of oatmeal to the table, stepped around the dog, and sat down with my quilt draped over my lap. Witch Boy hadn't said a word all during the banging and clattering of the bee pan. He picked his own times when he wanted to bark and when he didn't.

"Got us two nice jars of honey while they were out of the hive," Mawmaw said, glancing at the honey bowl on the table. "Lily Claire, you can take this big jar with the honeycomb in it to your daddy. Sam loves honey. Just like Jasper."

"Where's Papa Jasper?" I asked, drizzling a big spoonful of golden honey over my biscuit.

Mawmaw sat down at the table and glanced balefully at Witch Boy, who was running his wet black nose back and forth against the edge of the table, with his big brown eyes locked on the biscuit in my hand.

26

"He's gone off a'ramblin'. Said he was going turkey hunting. You know what that means. He'll stay gone all day and come home laughing with a funny story to tell about how he saw a tribe of turkeys marching along in a line, talkin' to each other!"

Willie T. snorted, blowing biscuit crumbs across the table. "Uncle Jasper's a fine man," he managed to declare, spouting more biscuit crumbs and honey. "I like to listen to his turkey stories."

"Well, he'll have one today. It's turning back warm out there, and it's sunny and clear. Believe that frost last night was just a cold snap, and it looks like we're goin' to have a pretty Indian Summer day. You younguns better get out and play while you can. We'll have a few days warm, then hit'll turn back cold, I vow. Ain't no tellin' which way the cat'll jump."

Willie T. and I listened to Mawmaw's prognostication while we finished up with breakfast.

"Speakin' of cats," she continued, "Lucinda has gone off somewhere to find kittens. Two days ago, and hasn't come back till yet. I've called her till I'm hoarse. It's goin' to be such a pretty day out there, I'll fix you younguns some sandwiches and a jar of tea, and why don't y'all go out and have you a picnic, and see if you can find her for me? I expect she's not far off, just out in the thicket somewhere under a bush. I'll walk down the hill and tell Sam and Sara where you've gone."

So after breakfast, my cousin and I put on our sweaters, picked up our brown paper sacks filled with fried baloney sandwiches, leftover biscuits, and Ball Mason jars full of tea, and headed out into the woods to look for Mawmaw's cat, Lucinda. We both speculated that Witch Boy might be a good cat locator if he could keep his mind off our sandwiches.

The three of us, without a care in the world, set off down the mountain road, headed no place in particular. Willie T. and I called "Kitty, kitty, kitty. Lucinda? Here kitty, kitty,

kitty!" as we strolled along the winding trail called Moor's Gap Road. Wouldn't you know it, Willie T. went to singing his most recent favorite song, "Would You Like to Go to Meetin' Uncle Joe," and I couldn't help singing along as we followed the winding dirt track.

Would you like to go to meetin', Uncle Joe, Uncle Joe
Would you like to go to meetin', Uncle Joe, Uncle Joe
Would you like to go to meetin', Uncle Joe, Uncle Joe
Don't' mind the weather when the wind don't blow

Will your horse carry double, Uncle Joe, Uncle Joe
Will your horse carry double, Uncle Joe, Uncle Joe
Will your horse carry double, Uncle Joe, Uncle Joe
Don't mind the weather when the wind don't blow

Hop up my ladies, two in a row
Hop up my ladies, two in a row
Hop up my ladies, two in a row
Don't mind the weather when the wind don't blow

Did you ever meet the devil, Uncle Joe, Uncle Joe
Did you ever meet the devil, Uncle Joe, Uncle Joe
Did you ever meet the devil, Uncle Joe, Uncle Joe
Don't mind the weather when the wind don't blow

Would you like to go to meetin', Uncle Joe, Uncle Joe
Would you like to go to meetin', Uncle Joe, Uncle Joe
Would you like to go to meetin', Uncle Joe, Uncle Joe
Don't' mind the weather when the wind don't blow

We were singing merrily as we rounded a big curve in the road, and just as we came up beside a big mound of tangled vines and underbrush, Witch Boy whirled around and started barking at the bushes.

"Meow," was the querulous reply from the thicket.

"Bark, bark, bark!"

"Meow?"

Willie T. looked at me expectantly, with his eyeballs out on stems and his eyebrows raised up nearly to the top of his head. "Listen there! I bet you a dollar and a half, that's ol' Lucinda."

We put our lunch sacks on a big log beside the dirt road, and slowly worked our way into the dense tangle of hedge bushes, vines, weeds, and briars, following the direction of the cat's meows. After getting just a little ways into the mess, we found that we couldn't stand up and make any further progress, so we ended up crawling on our hands and knees, weaving our way through the briars and hedges, with Witch Boy crawling along beside us.

"Where's that dad-blamed cat?" Willie T. grunted. He was answered by another distant meow.

"What's she doin' now? Don't let her get away from us. Where's she leadin' us to?"

I had to admit that I wondered the same thing. "Maybe she's leadin' us to her kittens," I suggested, hoping I was right. "Lucinda!" I called. "Kitty, kitty, kitty."

We followed the meows on through the jungle-like thicket, and out the other side into a clearing of sorts. There sat Lucinda in a patch of sunlight on a low, crumbling rock wall, washing her face and waiting for us. Me and Willie T. and Witch Boy hesitated, crouched on the ground in our forward-ho crawling position, and Lucinda gazed at us just a second or two, then jumped off the wall and scooted under a clump of tangled honeysuckle vines. As soon as the mama cat disappeared into the hiding place, we heard the sweet, high-pitched mewing of baby kittens.

"Found 'em!" Willie T. exclaimed as he popped up and began picking twigs and dead leaves out of his bristly head of hair. "That was purty easy."

29

I stood up and brushed my hands through my hair, dislodging an abundance of trash and vegetation. Witch Boy sat and began ceremoniously scratching his ear with his hind foot, then he flopped onto his back and started wiggling back and forth in the dust like a wiggle worm.

We found Lucinda under the old honeysuckle vines, sure enough, with five beautiful, tiny newborn kittens. There were two solid gray ones, and three just like Lucinda, white with gray spots. The kittens' little eyes were closed tight, and they weaved and bobbed around as Lucinda started grooming her babies, licking their fur and purring loud enough to beat the band.

"Aw," Willie T. crooned. "They're purty babies, Lucindy! Why'd you want to find 'em way out here in the thicket for?"

Lucinda purred and chirped happily, then plopped down among her tiny babies who immediately began looking for their dinner.

"I'm starved half to death!" my cousin announced. "While those kittens are gettin' their ninny, let's eat! Then we'll gather 'em all up and head back." Looking around at the dense brush we had come through, he groaned, "I hope we don't have to go back through them damned briars, though."

"Our lunch sacks are back there beside the road where we left them," I reminded him.

"If a panther ain't ate 'em up," Willie T. interjected.

"Maybe there's an easier way back," I suggested. We turned around a few times, surveying the lay of the land, and discovered that there was an old track, something like a wagon trail, leading back toward the road.

"Dang! Lookee there! We could'a come up that trail if we'd gone on down the road just a little bit! Look at that, Witch Boy! You led us all through that briar patch for nothin'!"

Witch Boy wagged his long tail and looked pretty proud of his tracking skills.

"You stay here with the kittens, and I'll go find our lunch

sacks. Don't let Lucinda carry them babies off anywheres," Willie T. cautioned as he trotted out of sight around a bend in the dirt trail.

I sat down on the vine-covered rock wall and Witch Boy laid his brown head on my lap, keeping his eyes trained on Lucinda and her tiny babies. I ran my hand along the rough surface of the ancient-looking rocks, and began to wonder what sort of building we had found. I had never heard anything about an old house or building of any kind being down here on this side of Moor's Gap Road, the sandy, unpaved road that ran from one side of Moonlight Ridge to the other.

It's hard to say exactly what happened next, as I sat petting Witch Boy with one hand and feeling the contours of the rock wall with the other hand. But suddenly my back stiffened with the creepy feeling that someone, or something, was watching me. The dog lifted his head quickly and made a little sound that was part growl and part whimper. He looked past me, and raised his nose into the air to sniff the breeze.

With a feeling of dread, I twisted around to look behind me. I sat stiff as a board and as still as a mouse, peering into the thick woods and cutting my eyes all around, this way and that.

There was no one behind me that I could see. But Witch Boy had started thumping the ground with his stupid old tail, the way he does when he sees somebody.

"Who is it, buddy?" I whispered. "Did you see somebody back there?"

The dog let loose with one sudden bark, a sharp, loud greeting that nearly made me have a heart attack. I looked back toward the woods behind me, in the direction Witch Boy was staring, and I declare, I thought I saw some sort of movement, maybe somebody in a long black dress, or maybe it could have been a black panther, looking for something else after eating up our lunches, for all I knew. Just a glimpse of something dark and shadowy that quickly moved out of

31

sight, back into the woods.

"Here you go," Willie T. announced right in my ear, thrusting a paper sack in my face and about causing me to have another heart attack!

I snatched the paper sack out of his hand, and I guess he saw the look on my face.

"What is it? You look like you seen a ghost."

"I thought I saw something behind those trees," I answered. "And Witch Boy acted like he saw something too."

Willie T. sat down beside me on the rock wall, and stared out at the forest.

"Gyah," he breathed. "I felt like it was somebody follerin' me all the way down that trail, and all the way back up here, too. Just a creepy feelin' …"

We both listened to the autumn wind passing through the trees.

"You don't' reckon it was that loup-garou, do you?"

A chill went down my back. "Or the wolfeener," I added, thinking about the terrible beast that roamed the mountain, making the scariest noise you could ever imagine.

Witch Boy impatiently nudged the lunch sack in my hand with his wet black nose.

"Well, whatever it was," I surmised, "*he* didn't seem to be worried none. Could'a been somebody just passin' by."

Willie T. didn't look convinced. "Yeah, could'a been," he answered. "Could'a been just somebody passin' by. The Possum Man, maybe. Joe John Lee. He lives out here somewheres, you know. Daddy said so. Lives out here with a whole bunch of possums in a possum den, 'cause he's so mean won't nobody let him live nowhere else. Mean as the devil. He just crawls in and out like a possum."

I sure hated to have to be the one to tell Willie T. that he didn't have the most up-to-date news concerning the Possum Man.

"I believe that the Possum Man's dead, Willie T. Died a long time ago … maybe last winter. Daddy said the sheriff found him … in some awful shape, all rotted away from bein' dead so long."

"Really? Possum Man's dead?" Willie T. asked, incredulous.

"I think so. That's what Daddy said."

Willie T. looked like he was about to cry. "Gyaah! Well, I'll be dad-gum! Poor ol' Possum Man," he sighed, shaking his head. "Poor ol' Possum Man!" he repeated. "I guess it just goes to show you."

I agreed that it surely did.

We opened up our paper sacks and ate fried boloney sandwiches, cold biscuits full of grape jelly, and drank the fruit jars of tea. Witch Boy watched us anxiously, so we fed him a few bites of our sandwiches and one whole jelly biscuit. Meanwhile, Lucinda passed the time licking and grooming her kittens. The hair on the back of my neck kinda stood up when Willie T. started absent-mindedly singing in a soft creepy voice.

"Did you ever meet the devil, Uncle Joe, Uncle Joe?
Did you ever meet the devil, Uncle Joe, Uncle Joe?"

I stared at him as hard as I could, and watched as he yawned and rubbed his eyes, smearing a fair amount of grape jelly and baloney grease on his cheeks. The way the sun looked, it was about one o'clock, and the day was turning warm and comfortable. Willie T. pulled off his nappy brown sweater and rolled it into a ball.

"This sunshine's puttin' me to sleep," he announced as he looked around for an apt place for a good nap. He sat down in the warm red sand and continued rolling and punching his wool sweater.

"Reckon what kind of a place this is?" he mused, glancing at the tumbled down rock walls. Along the slope of the hill and down toward the dirt trail, some of the walls were higher than our heads, as tall as the sides of a house. "Make a good

33

play-house, if we can get rid of some of these dang weeds." He yawned again. "I bet we could get some old kitchen chairs, an' a washtub for a table …"

I gave in to the warm sunshine and the hypnotic rhythm of Willie T.'s voice.

Five

Someone Watching

What woke me up was the sound of footsteps on the ground, right beside my ear.

"My scholars," an amused sounding voice came from somewhere on high.

Startled awake, the three of us, Willie T., Witch Boy, and me, jerked up to a sitting position, all three of us slack-jawed and flustered. The dog couldn't decide whether to bark, whine, or pant, so settled for shaking his head furiously, slinging an abundance of slobber in all directions.

"Gyah!" Willie T. protested, anxiously swiping at his slobber-sprinkled arms and face.

I squinted up at the apparition above us, the bemused face of our dear teacher, Erskine Batson.

"What in the world are y'all doing way out here in the lush countryside?" he asked with a sarcastic flourish.

"Th' lush countryside, my hind foot!" Willie T. replied. "More like Br'er Rabbit's dad-blamed briar patch!"

Erskine chuckled, lifting both hands up toward the blue sky in an exaggerated shrug. "Be that as it may," he commented nonchalantly. "I assume y'all are dreaming about that geometry test tomorrow, and just taking a brief re-spite from your studies."

"Geometry!" Willie T. exclaimed. "My daddy said we cain't learn no dang geometry in the dang fourth grade!"

Erskine moved over to the crumbling wall and sat down in the last little spot of sunshine, raking one eyebrow up as he studied our surroundings.

"Is your daddy the teacher?" he asked.

"Naw, he ain't," my cousin answered, unrepentant.

"Naw, he ain't," Erskine repeated. "I'm the teacher. Duly appointed. And I say we're studyin' geometry. Don't you fret none. You'll find the science of geometry to be a great help in many aspects of life, as the years go rolling by."

He leaned forward with his forearms resting on his knees, and spit on the ground. I don't know why men always spit on the ground, but they do. It seems to aid in the workings of their brain, somehow.

"Lily Claire, your daddy's the best brick layer in this county, right? And you know what? He uses geometry ever' time he lays one brick to another. Right angles and plumb lines and measurements and so on. You got to be smart to take a load of red brick and turn it into a magnificent building. Right?"

I thought about the precise lines of my daddy's brickwork, the way he tapped each brick as he placed it accurately in line with the others, and the rhythm of how he worked. Slap a trowel full of wet mortar down, a wedge of mortar at the end of the brick, lay it down and tap it into place. Then swipe the trowel across to remove the excess mortar that oozes out. Daddy called it mud.

"So that's how you use geometry?" I asked, suddenly intrigued. "Layin' brick?"

Erskine smiled. "That, and many other ways," he said.

"Well, I ain't plannin' to be no brick layer!" Willie T. spoke up. "Lily C.'s daddy lured me into helpin' him build a set of brick porch steps. Nearly worked me to death totin' bricks. I'm gonna play baseball."

Erskine studied my cousin for a few seconds.

"That will involve physics," he said. "We'll get to that."

Lucinda appeared and rubbed up against Erskine's pants leg in the little spot of warm sunshine, and he absent mindedly petted her as he continued to gaze around at the woods surrounding us.

"And who might this be?" he asked. "Y'all bringing your four-legged friends out for a stroll through the woods on this lovely afternoon?"

"That's Lucinda. She's the reason we're out here to begin with," Willie T. answered. "She come off out here and found her kittens, and Aunt Laurie sent us lookin' for her, to bring her and the kittens home."

"Ah, a search and rescue mission," Erskine said. "Where's the kittens?"

I pointed toward the mass of honeysuckle vines. "They're over there under those vines. Five of them. Mawmaw will be glad we found them. She's fixed up a cardboard box in her kitchen, right beside the stove."

"And what about this fine dog? He's a rare lookin' feller. Where'd you find him?"

Witch Boy cast a loving gaze at Erskine and wagged his tail, like he knew we were talking about him.

"We found him out near Widder Woman Holler, a month or two ago," I explained. "He was all skinny and hungry and had a spring stuck to the end of his tail."

Erskine jerked his head back and let loose with a big loud laugh. "A spring?" he spluttered.

"Sure as the world," Willie T. replied. "Stuck tight as Uncle Dick's hat band, right on the end of his old tail. Lily Claire pulled it off, didn't you Lily C.? And it shot through the air like a rocket ship and disappeared! The Lord's truth."

"A *spring*?" Erskine looked back and forth at Willie T. and me. "I swun, you two can tell the wildest tales I've ever heard."

"Lord's truth," Willie T. repeated.

"We named him Witch Boy," I added. "Because Willie T. thought it was a witch put that spring on the end of his tail. I don't know where he got any such of an idea as that."

Just then a big commotion started out in the woods, right about where I thought I had seen something moving earlier. All three of us jumped up and looked at the place where the noise had come from. Lucinda slunk down close to the ground and scooted back under the bushes with her kittens, and Witch Boy let out a long, happy sounding "Woo-woo, woo-woo, woof!"

I knew for sure someone was out in the woods watching us.

"Somebody's out there," I said. "That's Witch Boy's happy bark. It's the way he greets somebody, the way he says hello."

We all stood still and stared at the woods. It sounded like someone was walking close by, twigs cracking, then silence.

"I can't see anybody out there," Erskine said.

"I saw somebody — or something — while ago," I told him. "Something dark. Might have been somebody ... in a black dress."

"And I thought somebody was follerin' me down the trail while ago, too," Willie T. added ominously.

"I've always heard there's spooks out here in the gap," Erskine told us. "Moor's Gap. This here's the old stage coach stop," he said, "Been here since way back yonder. Since time immemorial."

"Stage coach? You mean like in a Roy Rogers movie?" Willie T. asked. "With a strongbox full of money and all?"

"Somethin' like that," Erskine answered. "All the old folks say there's haints aound this old stage coach inn. Nobody hardly comes out here much." He paused, then hollered, "Anybody out there?"

A few more twigs snapped.

Encouraged by Erskine's yelling, Witch Boy let out another joyful howl.

"Hush up, dog," I scolded. "You're gonna scare Lucinda and her babies."

"I'm ready to leave," Willie T. announced with a sudden shiver. "Let's get those kittens and skee-daddle."

My cousin and I tied our sweaters around our waists like aprons to carry the kittens home. I took three little babies and Willie T. took the other two. Lucinda watched us, but didn't seem to have any objections to us carrying her newborn kittens.

Erskine picked up our empty paper sacks and the iced tea jars.

"I'll walk back with y'all," he said, then he stopped abruptly and glanced back into the woods.

"Look," he whispered. "There ..."

I looked in the direction that Erskine was looking, and at first I didn't think I saw anything at all. Just trees and bushes moving with the wind. Lucinda circled around our feet, rubbing against my legs and purring, until Witch Boy commenced barking really loud. The racket scared the cat and caused her to arch her back and hiss like a wild cat.

Then I saw something. Or at least I thought I did. I caught a glimpse of something moving and heard the bushes rustling and it made me think of a bobcat, or a mountain lion. Or a panther.

"Lord a'mercy," Willie T. exclaimed. "What was that? Is it somebody watchin' us?"

We all stood quietly listening, but there wasn't another sound from the woods.

"All right," Erskine announced. "I think it's time for us to get on away from here. Look. Sun's going down. Let's us hurry on home."

And that's what we did.

Willie T. and I carried the babies and Lucinda followed

close behind, with Witch Boy trailing along, nose in the dust. Erskine cast his eyes back down the trail behind us more than once, but nothing seemed to be following us. By the time the bunch of us got back to Mawmaw's house, Erskine in the lead, me and Willie T. carrying our precious cargo with Lucinda weaving in and out around our feet, and Witch Boy bringing up the rear, darkness had descended on Moonlight Ridge.

Mawmaw met us at the back porch and held the screen door open for us to bring the kittens in.

"I found these two sound asleep out in the woods, layin' on the ground amid the leavings of their midday meal," Erskine informed her with no lack of sarcasm. "If I'd a'been a catamount, or a big black panther, or a bear for the lord's sake, they'd be eat up, total, instead of standin' here before you."

Mawmaw, still holding the screen door open, scrutinized the lanky, scruffy looking fellow standing on her back porch.

"Erskine Batson, there are no bears on Moonlight Ridge. I believe you'd have to go clean to Tennessee to see a bear."

"Be that as it may," he replied. "You need to teach them a little common sense. It ain't that safe for two younguns to be sprawled on the ground, devil-may-care, takin' a nap out on Moor's Gap."

"Hey, that rhymes!" Willie T. chirped.

"Moor's Gap!" Mawmaw exclaimed. "Law, is that where you found my kittens?" She turned her attention to Lucinda who was waiting patiently on the door jamb for us to get her babies situated.

"Lucindy! Why did you go way out there to find those babies? Law, law.

"And you." Mawmaw cast a none-too-respectful look at Erskine. "You're the teacher, ain't you?"

"That I am," he answered proudly. "Duly appointed. I feel like I've had this conversation once today already."

"Well, then, it's up to you to teach *these* two how to behave. They've growed up wild; from the time they could walk, they've been wild. But smart. They do okay, as long as they don't beat the stuffins out of each other."

Willie T. and I looked at each other.

"I witnessed no fisticuffs," Erskine volunteered. "Snorin' was more like it."

He handed the two empty Mason jars and the crumpled paper sacks to my Mawmaw. "But I reckon all's well that ends well. I'll bid you good evening, then," he added formally, stooped over and placed one hand on the edge of the wooden porch and jumped off, landing gracefully on the ground below.

"Geometry tomorrow," we heard him call from the darkness as he strolled out of sight.

"Peculiar boy," Mawmaw clucked. "Gone off to that college, and come back peculiar." She looked at the empty jars and greasy paper sacks in her hands. "Still pickin' up garbage, I see."

I figured she could have been talkin' about the discarded paper sacks, or she could have been talkin' about me and Willie T.

It was getting late, and Willie T. and I needed to get on home and get ready for school the next day. We put the five tiny mewing kittens in the cozy cardboard box with their mama, gave Mawmaw a good-night hug, then ran at top speed down the hill to my house, with Witch Boy yipping and nipping at our heels.

Mama was on the front porch, standing under the porch light and flapping the white dish towel in her hands like a flag of truce.

"Willie T. Nock, your mama has already called twice on the telephone looking for you. You get on home now. Don't make Rachel nervous."

"Yes'm," Willie T. answered quickly, and trotted on down the dirt road toward his house.

"See you tomorrow, Lily C.," he called from the distance.

At the supper table I told Mama and Daddy all about the week-end my cousin and I had spent at Mawmaw's house. All about Papa's scary loup-garou tale, and how the wind blew the front door open and scared us all half to death. When I told about Papa playing his guitar and singing about the virgin just nineteen years old, my daddy laughed out loud and clapped his hands.

I told them that me and Willie T. went off in the woods and found Lucinda's kittens and brought them home to Mawmaw's house.

But I didn't tell them about how we thought somebody had been watching us in the woods, or how we heard someone walking and thought we saw someone, or something, moving through the bushes around us. It gave me a funny feeling every time I started to mention it, so I just let it pass.

But that night, snuggled in my soft warm bed, I thought about it over and over before I went to sleep, and the more I thought, the more I believed I actually had seen someone watching us. I don't know why, but somehow I got it in my head that it might have been a ghost. A haint, as Erskine had said, on Moor's Gap Road. The darkness outside my bedroom window looked as thick as black ink before I closed my eyes and pulled the cover over my head.

We have always lived with ghosts on Moonlight Ridge. Out on the mountain, ghostly happenings are simply an everyday occurrence. Like an old church house you see one day out in the woods, and it's not there the next day. And like the old widow woman who haunts Widder Woman Holler, with her goat that talks to her out in the dark. And like having to remember to take the dipper out of Mawmaw's metal water bucket before you go to bed, or else it'll whirl round and round making a terrible racket all night long. Mawmaw says it's the ghost of John Henry, the railroad man, coming in to get a drink of water. We've never laid eyes on him, or his ghost. We've just seen the dipper whirling round and round, and heard the awful screeching noise it makes as it scrapes around in the water bucket.

But that night as I was falling asleep, I felt certain that I had seen a dark girl in the woods at the old stage coach stop, and I had a scary feeling that she just might be the first ghost I had ever actually laid eyes on, face to face.

Monday morning, the weather had turned off cold again, just like Mawmaw warned us it would, and we all arrived at school shivering and chapped by the wind. I envied all the boys in their long blue jeans and overalls. All us girls weren't allowed to wear pants to school, and like most of the other girls in the fourth grade, I'd had a growing spurt so all my dresses were too short to cover my legs. Mama had gone shopping at Robert Hall's, and bought me a red wool coat with a hood to pull up over my head, so that helped some. But rest assured, a coat with a hood leaves somethin' to be desired when there's an icy wind blowin' up your skirt tail.

Mr. Erskine, which is what we had to call him in the classroom, made good on his promise to deliver a geometry test first thing in the morning, right after we finished doing our eyeball exercises. But we all made a perfect score because he did the problems with us on the blackboard so everybody could see how to figure out the answers, which mostly amounted to using our colored plastic protractors to measure this angle and that. Mr. Erskine said this would do us a world of good someday later on in life, and that we owed an eternal debt to somebody named Euclid for coming up with the whole geometry business way back in the dark ages. We all agreed that we wished Mr. Euclid had found some other way to pass the time, like digging in the dirt or singin' "Somewhere Over the Rainbow" with Mr. Pythagorus.

Halloween was coming up in just a few days, Wednesday, October 31st, right in the middle of the week, and we were all excited about that. Miss Puck, the sweet little county music teacher, came around and gave each one of us an orange lollipop with a jack-o-lantern face on it, then taught us a spooky Halloween song about a headless phantom leaping around in the pumpkin patch!

After she had us totally terrified with that shivery song, she said goodbye, blushing and smiling in Mr. Erskine's direction as she drifted out of our classroom and disappeared down the hallway. Erskine stood leaning against his desk for about a minute, gazing down the long hallway where Miss Puck had disappeared, with some kind of half-amused smile on his face. Then he suddenly straightened up, cleared his throat loudly, and got back to business as usual.

He passed out great big sheets of heavy manila drawing paper and black boxes of fragrant Crayola crayons, and showed us how to draw a line of orange pumpkins sitting on a picket fence, with a big yellow moon and ghostly looking white clouds in the sky. Then we painted over our pictures with stinky black tempera paint, and right before our astonished eyes, our clumsy crayon drawings turned into real works of art. We were all impressed with ourselves.

Play period was a trial, with most of us running around the playground like crazy people, just trying to keep moving enough so we didn't freeze solid. You didn't dare to touch the icy cold metal swing frames or the monkey bars if you had any sense at all. There was always some lame-brained big boys from the sixth grade trying to convince some first or second grader to stick his tongue to the freezing cold monkey bars. But even the little kids had been warned by their older brothers and sisters not to do it, even though the temperature wasn't really cold enough to make their tongues stick. But the big sixth grade boys never gave up trying, and seemed to fall into despair of all human nature when they couldn't convince even one single first grader to go along with their evil game.

My mama had told me that when she and Aunt Rachel were little, the kids used to dare each other to stick their tongues to the freezing cold railroad tracks that ran through

John Henry's haunted tunnel on the side of the mountain! She said if the weather was cold enough, your tongue really would stick to the steel rails, just like sticking to an ice cube out of the Frigidaire. And then all the other kids would run away laughing and leave you there by yourself, waiting for the ghost of John Henry to sneak up on you. Just the thought of it sort of filled me with dread every time the weather got cold!

That whole week before Halloween passed pretty much the same, with all the students singing the spooky Halloween Visitor song, all the teachers trying to come up with new and exciting ways to use crayons and stinky black paint to create works of art, and everybody doing their best not to die of frost bite.

Our principal, Mr. Vales, still looking just like a black crow with his slick black hair, bushy black eyebrows, and black beady eyes, visited each and every classroom and checked to make sure every student had some manner of a coat to wear. And if he discovered somebody without sufficient attire for the bad weather, he rummaged around in the lost-and-found cloak room and brought out whatever he could find. Many a child had Mr. Vales to thank for a holey wool jacket and a raveled knit toboggan cap.

The principal caught Erskine in the hallway one gray afternoon when he tried to leave with just a threadbare flannel shirt covering his lanky frame. Mr. Vales took off his own black wool coat and made the flustered young teacher take it.

"You wear this for a few days, Erskine, till the weather gets better," Mr. Vales insisted. "I got more coats than I know what to do with."

"I can't take your coat, Principal Vales," Erskine protested. "But I appreciate the offer, all the same."

"No, now, you *can* take it. I said so, didn't I? You can watch me go right in my office and pull another coat off the coat rack, just as good as this one. And a scarf and gloves and my hat! My wife bundles me up like a mummy ever' time the wind blows!" He chuckled and patted Erskine's gaunt shoulder a time or two.

"You take this coat, now, and keep warm. I'll never miss it."

Then Principal Vales glanced at me and Willie T. standing there google-eyed, watching the whole proceedings, and he winked at us with a sly little smile. And that's how Erskine got a long black coat for the winter and it's how me and Willie T. learned that old Crow Face Vales was really a generous, kind-hearted man.

Six

Halloween

The houses on Moonlight Ridge are too far apart to do much good at trick-or-treating unless you want to walk yourself to death. And Mama and Daddy insisted that we go out while it was still daylight, so we wouldn't be traipsing around in the dark. Especially that year because on the last night of October there was a new moon, which meant no moon at all, which meant a pitch black night.

As soon as I got home from school I dressed up in the warmest clothes I could find, topped by a pointed witch's hat made out of black construction paper and a little black mask from V.J. Elmore's ten-cent store. By the time I was ready to go, Willie T. met me at the front door, dressed in an array of raggedy clothes and a bright green paper mask covering his face.

"Frankenstein!" he growled in a menacing voice, holding his hands up in the air like giant claws.

We both squealed and giggled and chased each other around the front porch, causing Witch Boy to set in barking and running after us.

Mama opened the screen door and called the dog to her.

"Witch Boy! Come here, boy! I've got something for you." And she placed a little black cone of construction paper on his silly old brown head, held in place by a string of brown twine tied in a tight bow under his chin. Witch Boy squeezed his eyes shut and stood still while she adjusted the miniature witch's hat on top of his head, then he made us all laugh when he scampered around the porch, circling us in a wild race! The little black hat stayed securely on his head.

"Y'all go on now, and get back here before dark," Mama said, wiping tears from her eyes from laughing at the dog.

She told us that Willie T.'s parents, Aunt Rachel and Uncle Buddy Nock, were coming for supper, as she handed us two brown paper lunch sacks to hold whatever trick-or-treat candy we collected. The bags were small and we knew it would be slim pickins, with only three or four houses in walking distance. But Willie T. and I were good walkers, and we were as excited as if we were off on a treasure hunt.

After making the rounds, what we ended up with was a handful of Tootsie Rolls from my Mawmaw Laurie and Papa Jasper, a handful of orange and yellow candy corn from Uncle Junebug Isbell, some crumbly Graham Crackers from Mrs. Myrtle Batson, Erskine's mother, where we were surprised to get anything at all considering her house full of younguns, and on down the road a whole Hershey Bar for each of us from Estaleen Howard, Erskine's sister. At Estaleen's house we were pretty well terrified by the sight of her husband, Cowboy, running around their house with a paper sack over his head, leaping through the air and howling like the wolfeener, while Estaleen, looking a little put out, came to the door to give us our Hershey Bars. She was holding their sweet little baby, Junior, who was laughing and kicking, and seemed to be totally delighted by the sight of his daddy bounding through the house and cuttin' the fool like a crazy man.

So on this Halloween afternoon, with our meager bounty jostling in our brown paper sacks, the three of us, Willie T., Witch Boy, and me, found ourselves meandering down the road with time on our hands.

"Let's go ahead and eat them Graham Crackers," Willie T.

suggested, pushing his green Frankenstein mask up on top of his head.

"I don't really like Graham Crackers," I said, still wearing my black witch hat and my ten-cent-store mask.

"I know it," my cousin replied. He reached into his trick-or-treat bag and extracted an irregular shaped shard of sugary Graham Cracker. "But they're gettin' all broke up in the bottom of the sack. Makin' a mess."

We sat on a fallen log beside the red dirt road and nibbled the dry, crumbling morsels, which Witch Boy devoured with enthusiasm. So far, none of us had come across anything edible that Witch Boy would cull.

Willie T. held a triangular shaped piece of Graham Cracker under his nose and sniffed loudly.

"I don't know why you don't like these," he puzzled. "Smells spicy."

"Too dry," I complained, still crunching a mouthful of crumbs and sugar. "And too spicy."

Willie T. giggled, then recited in an artificially serious voice, "Ever'thing smells right spicy!"

I blinked and stared at my companion with the green Frankenstein mask perched on top of his bristly flat-top.

"You remember that story, don't you?" he asked. "Ever'thing smells right spicy?"

I foresaw that he was about to launch into his story telling mode.

"It was way back, a long time ago, when Great Granddaddy W.T. Greenberry and Great Grandmother Augusta had all their kinfolks a'visitin' for Thanksgiving. They had so many people all over the house, there was people piled up sleepin' everywhere. There was Greenberrys and Leverts and Isbells and I don't know who all. Might a' been some Nashes and Nocks.

"Old Uncle Sefton Isbell and old Grandpaw Percival Greenberry was sleepin' on pallets on the dining room floor. And old Grandpaw Percival Greenberry had to get up in the middle of the night, and he told Uncle Sefton he had to go outside, and Uncle Sefton said on such a cold dark night he was glad it wasn't him that had to go out. So the old man said, seein' as how cold it was, he thought instead of walkin' all the way to the out-house, he'd just open the back door and pee-pee off the side of the portico."

I stopped chewing my mouthful of Graham Cracker and elbowed my cousin as hard as I could.

"Quit it!" Willie T. snapped. "That's what he said!"

"And bein' in a strange place in the middle of the night, the old man groped around and felt his way along in the dark till he found what he thought was the back door. But in the pitch black dark, he'd opened up the wrong door and he stepped into the dark kitchen pantry, and it was so cold in there, he thought he was outside on the porch, and he peed in the spice pantry!

"Well, he come shiverin' back into the dark dining room and crawled back under the covers on the floor, and Uncle Sefton Isbell asked him, 'Well, how's the weather out there? Has it commenced to rainin' or sleetin' yet?' And Grandpaw Percival anwered him, 'No, not yet. Not a drop of rain in sight! It's clear as a bell, cold as hell, and everything smells right spicy!' "

Willie T. rocked back and forth on the log we were sitting on, laughing and pushing me till I fell off the log.

"Ever'thang smells right spicy!" he cried in a fit of laughter.

Of course, he'd already made my giggle box turn over, and I spluttered Graham Cracker crumbs all over the place, which caused Witch Boy to cut loose barking as loud as he could possibly bark. With me and Willie T. both having a laughing fit and Witch Boy barking like a lunatic, it was a pure melee. Willie T. sprawled out on his back, kicked the log with both his feet, and yelled to the sky, "Ever'thang smells right spicy!"

And that's how Erskine found us.

"What in the world are y'all up to now?" he asked, standing over us, elbows akimbo and hands on his hips.

Witch Boy bared his teeth and lurched toward the teacher's legs, but quickly sniffed out who it was and started wagging his tail instead of biting.

Giving the dog a withering glance, Erskine continued. "First I find you sound asleep in the arboreal forest, and now I come upon you in the throws of hysterical abandon, side of the road. Ain't y'all got any style of decorum about you?"

I blushed at being reprimanded by our teacher, and straightened up my tall black witch's hat the best I could. Willie T., meanwhile, remained on his back with his feet against the log and peered up at Erskine's face high above us.

"It's just that ever'thang smells right spicy!" he exclaimed and burst into a new peal of laughter.

Erskine smiled just a little.

"I've heard that story," he admitted. "It's a little off color, if you ask me."

He turned and sat down on the log, brushing Willie T.'s feet out of the way. Reaching in the pocket of Mr. Vales' black wool coat, he pulled out a pack of Lucky Strike cigarettes and a box of matches, lit a cigarette and blew a long stream of smoke out into the chilly autumn air.

"Well, did y'all get plenty of trick-or-treats?"

"Graham Crackers, candy corn, Tootsie Rolls, and Estaleen gave us both a whole Hershey Bar," Willie T. reported.

"Hershey Bar!" Erskine echoed. "Me too!" And he grinned and pulled a half-eaten chocolate bar out of his pocket.

"Good weather for Hershey Bars," he opined. "They're a mess in the summertime."

He stuffed his Lucky Strikes, matches, and half a Hershey Bar back into the coat pocket. Witch Boy wagged his tail some more and eyeballed the coat pocket.

"Well, scholars, I'm fixin' to walk back up the Moor's

Gap, take another look at that archaeological site y'all discovered." Erskine unfolded his lanky frame into a standing position and brushed a few twigs from his coat. "Feel like going along?"

Willie T. looked a little surprised and shrugged his shoulders.

"We got to be home by dark," I said.

"Yeah, we do," Willie T. agreed. "Aunt Sara said so."

"Up to you." Erskine threw down his cigarette butt on the sandy road and ground it out with his shoe. "I feel like looking around up there again. See what's what."

Willie T. and I quickly agreed to go. To tell the truth, we had both been itching to go back up there to investigate the old stage coach inn ourselves. We had talked it over at great length and made big plans for turning the tumbled down old remains into a secret club house. After discussing the eerie feelings we both had experienced on the day we were out there collecting Lucinda's kittens, we came to the consensus that it wasn't any scarier than spending the night at Mawmaw's house on a dark night with the bucket dipper spinning round and round.

So we set off up the sandy road, the tall black-coated teacher, me in a black witch's hat, Willie T. wearing a green Frankenstein mask on top of his head, and crazy old Witch Boy with his black hat dangling around his neck.

Due to the fact that the wind wasn't blowing, the chilly autumn air wasn't too uncomfortable, and walking uphill kept us warm. Not one to waste an occasion for oratory, Erskine seized the opportunity to tell us a little bit of what he'd been able to find out about Moor's Gap and the old stage coach inn.

He started out by explaining why the place was called Moor's Gap to begin with. We followed the dirt road higher and higher, then suddenly it dropped off into a little valley of sorts, with a high ridge of the mountains on each side. And it was right there where we found the trail that led up to the ruins of the old inn.

"See, it's called a gap because it's a path, or an opening, running in between the two high ridges of the mountain here. People and animals just naturally follow this trail because it makes it easier to cross the mountain. And," he added, making a wide sweeping motion toward the remnants of the old building, "it's called Moor's Gap for a reason. Who can tell me what a Moor is?"

He looked first at me, then at Willie T.

"A cow," my crazy cousin guessed.

Erskine looked appalled and shook his head. "No," he said.

"A place where you tie up your boat," was Willie T.'s next stab at it.

Our teacher heaved a burdensome sigh and shrugged his shoulders, and took off up the weedy path toward the tumbled down old walls of the ancient building.

"A Moor is a black man," he called back over his shoulder. "The Moors were from Spain, maybe originally from somewheres else, from Morocco maybe. A colorful race ..."

"Colored people," Willie T. surmised.

"Well, yes," Erskine answered. "But that's not what I meant by colorful. Colorful means ... very interesting. Like a colorful character. The history of the Moors is a long and colorful story. How one of 'em ended up here on Moonlight Ridge would be a revelation to know."

We reached the open dusty spot where Erskine had discovered me and Willie T. asleep in the sun on the day we found Lucinda and her kittens in the bushes.

"See, way back then, maybe a hundred years ago, a man they called a Moor ran this very stage coach inn, before there was any automobiles or trains through here. It was a stage coach line that ran from the east, right through here then down to Montevallo, then on down south to Mobile and New Orleans. Carried people where they needed to go, rich folks mostly, I imagine. And this was a place they could stop, rest and change horses, get something to eat and a bed for the night. I'd love to have seen it, the way it was back then."

While he rambled on with this information, Erskine had begun picking up and inspecting the heavy stones that lay scattered on the ground, then stacking them against what remained of the wall.

"This place is full of history," he told us, shaking his head a little. "Surprising that nobody seems to talk about it." He turned and looked at me, scratched the back of his head, then sat down on the low wall. "I found out what I know about it from your grandpaw, Lily Claire. Uncle Jasper Nash."

"Papa! He knows about this stage coach inn?" I asked.

"He sure does. Uncle Jasper knows everything there is to know about these woods. About this whole mountain. What he didn't learn as a boy, he learned from the old man, W.T. Greenberry."

"Great Granddaddy W.T.!" Willie T. exclaimed. "That's who I'm named after!"

"As the story goes," Erskine continued, "Uncle Jasper says there was a famous robber that hid out in these woods. He robbed the stage coach on several occasions, and always got away with it. Rode a beautiful Andalusian horse he'd bought from the Moor, the inn keeper. For years he pestered travelers on this road, stole gold and silver coins and jewelry."

My cousin and I were spellbound.

"Gyah!" Willie T. breathed. "Just like in the movies. Like Jesse James!"

Erskine nodded. "Something like that. But ..." He shook his head and smiled a sad-looking smile. "He finally got caught. A troop of soldiers was layin' for him out here in the woods, one night. Shot him right here, in front of the inn."

"Awww!" Willie T. protested.

"They called him the Highwayman," Erskine added as he snapped the stem off a dead weed and started scratching the back of his head with it. "Uncle Jasper says he'd never harmed a soul. Stole a bunch of loot, though. President James Buchanan his-self had put out a warrant for our Highwayman, put a bounty on his head, because of this being an important travel route down to the southern shipping ports."

It seemed to me like Erskine's tale had finally jogged something loose in my brain. "The Highwayman? I've heard Papa Jasper sing that song about the Highwayman! It's a sad song."

"Um hm," Erskine agreed, still scratching his head with the brown twig. "He sang that song for me just a few days ago, when I was pickin' at him for information. It's a sad tune, all right. But the song was originally copied from a poem written by an Englishman named Alfred Noyes, about a robber highwayman in old England. But it's so close to the same story that happened here, Uncle Jasper says when he was a boy, everybody thought the song was written about the Moor's Gap highwayman. The poem, too. A strange case of coincidence. King George's army killed the highwayman in England, and it was the local militia killed our highwayman here on Moor's Gap Road. Shot him dead, with his sweetheart lookin' on."

"Awww!" Willie T. said again.

Erskine sighed, threw down the dead weed he was holding, and turned to face me and my cousin.

"The moral of the story is, crime doesn't pay," he concluded.

Suddenly, something gave me a chill, like a possum had run over my grave. I looked around at the dense thicket of bushes surrounding us and the tall trees moving in the wind. A brilliant cascade of red and yellow and gold leaves showered down around us.

"I feel like it's somebody watchin' us," I whispered.

Witch Boy's ears went up as he stood and fixed his eyes on the woods up the hill.

"Me too," Willie T. said, shifting his eyes this way and that.

Mr. Erskine straightened up and looked around. We heard old Bu, the hoot owl, calling from somewhere far out in the woods, and a flock of big black crows flew over and landed in a tree beside us.

"It's gettin' late," Erskine told us. "I'd better get you young people home on this Halloween night."

Witch Boy chose that quiet moment to let loose a loud, nerve shattering series of barks. The crows left the tree with a noisy flapping of wings, their harsh raspy voices cawing and fussing as they went.

"Look here, it's about to get dark on us," Erskine announced. "We've stayed too long out here tellin' tales. We best hurry on down the mountain while there's still light enough to navigate."

"Come on, dog," he commanded, but Witch Boy ran off into the woods.

"He'll foller us," Willie T. assured our teacher. "You don't have to call him."

Erskine grabbed hold of our hands in an exuberant grip, me on one side and Willie T. on the other, took a deep breath and broke out singing the end of the Highwayman song in a strong and surprisingly pleasant voice.

"And still of a winter's night, they say, when the wind is in the trees ... "

And that's the last sound we heard before the ground disappeared from beneath our feet.

Seven

A Peculiar Predicament

The three of us, bunched close together and holding hands, had stepped over a patch of dead weeds onto a scattered pile of leaves, and found ourselves plummeting downward with nothing in the world under our feet but thin air. We hit the bottom of whatever we had fallen into with a disconcerting whump: arms, legs, coats, trick-or-treat bags, and Halloween costumes entangled.

Erskine Batson had landed flat on his back and the impact knocked the breath out of him. Willie T. and I had fared somewhat better, having landed right on top of our unfortunate teacher.

Erskine pitched forward, casting us aside roughly in a wild thrashing of long arms and kicking of long legs. We watched in horror as the suffocating man, his mouth gaping open like some terrible fish out of water, clutched desperately at his throat, then at his chest, then his throat again.

"God a'mighty," Willie T. exclaimed. "We've killed our teacher!"

The two of us immediately yielded to instinct and grabbed Erskine by the shoulders of his black wool coat, shaking him violently back and forth and at the same time pounding him on the back as hard as we could.

"Get his arms up," I yelled. "Hold his arms straight up over his head." And we each grabbed a flailing arm and

57

raised them over Erskine's head. Though the poor victim tried to fend us off, we kept shaking and pounding until, with a great noisy gasp, the teacher finally managed to suck wind.

He sat with his long legs bent and arms resting on his knees for about a minute, taking long shuddering breaths and taking note of our situation.

"We're in a hole," Willie T. glumly confirmed what the teacher was beginning to realize on his own.

Erskine took a few more deep breaths, raised up into a crouched position with his arms still braced on his knees, then echoed my cousin's earlier epithet.

"God a'mighty!"

He glanced around at our surroundings then turned his face up and gazed for a few seconds at the perfect circle of gray sky above us.

"Lord a'mighty," he moaned. Then he grabbed me first, then Willie T., running his hands over our heads and down our shoulders and backs.

"Are y'all all right? Are you hurt anywhere?"

We both reported that we were fine, shaking out our arms and legs and finding no sore spots. Erskine kicked at the thick carpet of leaves and pine straw at our feet and told us it had probably saved us from serious injury.

"Looks like we're in something of a peculiar predicament," he said, reaching high above his head and running his hands along the dirt wall surrounding us. "I swear, I've lived around these parts my entire life, and this is a new one on me! Far as I can recall, I don't think I know of anybody gettin' trapped in a hole in the ground before."

"Speak for your own durn self," Willie T. grumbled under his breath.

Erskine raised his eyebrows and shot a quizzical look at my cousin, but let it go.

"What we have here is a problem of physics. I'm about five foot eleven. I can reach up maybe a couple of feet above my head." He crouched and jumped up a couple of times, slapping the dirt wall above his head as he jumped. "Looks like we're in about a nine or ten foot hole."

He looked around, kicking at the pine straw. "Don't appear to be nothing to stand on to get me up any higher." He paused, looking up at the circle of pale sky above us. "And it's gettin' late."

Erskine folded his arms across his chest and silently stared at me and Willie T. for a few seconds. Then he pulled the two of us together, back to back. "Which one of y'all is the tallest?" he asked, discovering that we were pretty much exactly the same height. He grasped Willie T.'s shoulder.

"Well, my man, eenie-meanie-minie-mo. Looks like you're the one to go!

"I'm gonna squat down, and you climb up on my shoulders. I'll hold onto your legs and stand up. See if that gets you up high enough to pull yourself out."

And that's what they did. Erskine stood facing the wall of our dirt enclosure with the Frankenstein clad boy balanced, none too steady, on his shoulders.

"It's just like in the circus," Willie T. mused. He stretched upward and reached as high as he could toward the opening. "I can just about reach it," he grunted, arms extended above his head.

"Hey!" he suddenly yelled, jerking so that he almost lost his balance. Erskine shifted a little, readjusting his grip on Willie T.s legs.

"Hey!" Willie T. yelled again, then up he went, out of Erskine's grasp, and out of sight over the rim of the hole.

"What the ..." we heard his confused sounding voice from high above. Then a few seconds of silence.

My cousin's face, crowned by the green Frankenstein mask still perched on top of his head, appeared over the edge of the hole.

"Well, I'm out!" he exclaimed.

"What happened?" Erskine and I both asked at the same time.

The boy above us looked to his left and right, shaking his head.

"I don't know. It felt like somebody grabbed ahold of me and pulled me up. But ..." He paused and looked around again. "There ain't nobody up here that I can see."

We heard excited barking in the distance.

"Wait," Willie T. said. "Yonder comes Witch Boy."

The strident barking got closer, then Willie T.'s puzzled face leaning over the hole was joined by the jubilant brown face of our crazy dog, smiling and licking.

"Here, get off of me!" Willie T. protested. "They ain't nobody else around," he called down to us.

"Well," Erskine said, shrugging his shoulders and slapping his hands down to his sides. "Looks like it's your turn, Lily Claire. Can you climb out of here just like he did?"

"Sure she can," Willie T., still wrestling with the dog, answered for me. "She can do anythang I can do."

With that assurance, I climbed up onto our teacher's shoulders and balanced with my hands against the dirt wall as Erskine stood up slowly, holding a firm grip on my ankles. Willie T. reached down and grabbed both my hands and pulled while Erskine shoved from below, and I scrambled over the edge of the hole, dislodging a few clumps of dirt and weeds that fell onto the smiling teacher's upturned face.

Witch Boy barked gaily, abandoned his attacks on Willie T. and jumped on me, almost knocking me back into the hole.

Down in the hole, Erskine sent up a cheer.

"Bravo! Perfecto! Fait accompli! Okay, scholars! Now it's up to you two to figure out how to fish *me* out of here."

I lay on my stomach beside my cousin and the brown dog, and watched our teacher down at the bottom of the deep pit, hastily picking up the brown paper trick-or-treat sacks and all the spilled Halloween candy, stuffing it all into the pockets of his long black coat. He gazed up at us expectantly, and something about his trusting innocent face looked almost like a child, in trouble and needing help. I have to admit, I felt a little panicky.

"Look how dark it's gettin'," Willie T. sighed. The worried expression on his face mirrored my near-hopeless feeling. "We better hurry up and do somethin'.

"I got an idear!" he exclaimed. "We could drop a bunch of them big rocks down there, till there was enough for you to stand on and climb out!"

"Take too long," Erskine answered. "And you'd prob'ly drop one of them on my head and knock my brains out. Nah, y'all better come up with a better plan. Or run get help. Uncle Jasper ... or Sam Nash ..."

"Gyah!" Willie T. drawled. "Then we'll *all* be in trouble."

"Yeah, well." Erskine mumbled in the hole.

Willie T., deep in thought, pulled his Frankenstein mask down over his face, then pushed it back onto the top of his head and spit on the ground.

"We need to get Henry Hope," he said.

"Henry Hope? Henry Hope Nash?" Erskine exclaimed. "Why in the world?"

"He...uh...might could be of some help," Willie T. suggested. I knew exactly what he was thinking about. It was Henry Hope Nash, my daddy's very strange cousin, who had rescued Willie T. out of a similar situation when he fell into an old dried up well just a few months before. But nobody else but me and Willie T. and Henry Hope knew about that.

"It's a long walk to Henry Hope's house in Eden," I reminded him.

"Too long," Erskine shouted. "Y'all can't be runnin' all over the countryside in the dark, which it just about is. And I'd personally love to get out of this hole before midnight-thirty!"

"What about Cowboy Howard?" I suggested. "He's home from the sawmill —runnin' around the house with a paper sack on his head."

"Yes, he is," Erskine confirmed. "I was privileged to witness *that* spectacle earlier this evenin'."

"Good idear, Lily C.," Willie T. cheered. He leaned over the edge of the darkening hole. "Hold on down there. We're goin' to get Cowboy. Be right back."

"That's a comfort," Erskine answered, sounding pretty hopeless.

As we raced away from the pit, with Witch Boy gleefully leaping beside us, we could hear Erskine muttering from down below.

"I'll be here."

Eight

The Rescue

We ran at top speed, away from Moor's Gap and up the first rise.

"We need a long ladder," Willie T. speculated as we ran along the shadowy dirt road. "Or a rope."

"We need a miracle," I suggested. "Or some magic. We need Studebaker Freeman's magic stick." I waved my hand in front of his face, like waving a magic wand. "Abracadabra," I chanted.

Then the strangest thing in the world happened. Out on the mountain, with the sun gone down and twilight setting in, I guess you just have to be prepared for strange occurrences.

We ran headlong into Studebaker Freeman.

Willie T. and Witch Boy and I were running so fast, I guess we weren't looking out where we were going, and it seemed like Studebaker Freeman, a young black man who was crazy as a doodle bug and pretty much a celebrity in the town of Eden, just appeared out of nowhere. The four of us collided right in the middle of the road. The paper shopping bag that he was carrying sailed out of his hands and landed on the ground behind him. There was a definite sound of breaking glass.

Startled out of our wits, Willie T. and I both screamed as loud as we could and started thrashing around, trying to disentangle ourselves. Witch Boy lowered his head and flattened his ears, ready to attack. Sad to say, our dog wasn't fond of the eccentric Studebaker.

"Hey! Look what you done!" the exasperated man yelled. "My Co-Colas! Broke all to pieces, I expect!"

"Studebaker Freeman!" my cousin and I screeched at the same time.

Witch Boy circled.

"Getch'yo dog! Getch'yo dog," Studebaker repeated, pointing at the snarling animal with the short stick he carried in his hand. He was not fond of dogs.

I grabbed Witch Boy by his collar, gave him a good shake and told him to calm down, which he did. Then, wouldn't you know it, he started in wagging his old tail and yipping a friendly greeting, sincere or not.

Willie T. laid his hand over his heart, like he was about to have a pure-dee heart attack.

"Studebaker Freeman, what the Dickens are you doin' out here on the mountain?"

"Now, that's a good question. I'd like to know the answer to that question myself. Um hmm. I was home, hidin' out from the Halloween spooks, and didn't have no intentions about leaving my house tonight. Then, it seem like the Lord just spoke to me. Seem like all of a sudden I knew there was trouble up here somewhere, and I knew in my heart it was somebody out here in need of help. Um hmm! That's sure enough the truth. But I sure didn't expect it to be you two scalawag childrens, though. Runnin' down the road out here like the booger-man, and it might near dark! Broke my Co-Colas!"

With a feeling of relief and urgency, Willie T. and I grabbed hold of Studebaker like grabbing hold of a life raft in the middle of the ocean. Both of us were chattering a mile a minute, trying to explain the situation as we pulled the confused fellow back toward the hole where we'd left Erskine.

"Hold on a minute!" Studebaker insisted, raising his hands up in a gesture that meant 'stop this.'

"What in the world y'all tryin' to say? I can't listen to two folks at once. You two scalawag childrens, wear me to a frazzle!"

"Erskine's fell in a hole," Willie T. explained impatiently. "Really and truly. A big hole in the ground and we can't get him out."

"Erskine Batson? That teacher? That teacher drives the garbage truck?"

"Yes, our teacher! Fell in a big ol' deep hole," Willie T. yelped.

"He dead?" our rescuer asked, his eyes big around as baseballs.

"No, he's not dead," I assured him, still tugging at his sleeve with one hand and pushing Witch Boy back away from us with the other hand. "He's not hurt at all, just got the breath knocked out of him, is all."

"But we can't get him out," Willie T. added. "Hole's too deep. Come on, let's hurry!"

So off we went, tearing back down the road, me and Willie T. yelling "Hurry, hurry!" and the crazy dog barking and leaping, and Studebaker continuing to ask questions as we ran.

"How'd Erskine Batson get in a hole? How big is the hole? How long he been in that hole? He bound to require medical attention?"

We were nearing the place where we'd left Erskine in the hole when Studebaker stopped abruptly and peered around at the darkening woods. "Who's that I hear talking?" he whispered. "I heard somebody talking."

We stood still and listened, but I didn't hear anything.

"There's shades out here, tonight, sure enough. I tell you that's the truth," Studebaker whispered as we all took off running again.

We arrived back at the hole with evening gloom settling like a heavy black fog over the woods.

"Erskine, we got help," I called out.

"The thang is," Willie T. said to no one in particular, "we got to be home before dark."

Studebaker looked around skeptically at our gloomy surroundings, but made no reply to this announcement. He leaned cautiously over the edge of the hole and looked in.

"You down there? You down there talking to yourself or what?"

"Studebaker?" Erskine exclaimed from out of the deep.

"Yep, it's me all right. These childrens told me you was in a hole! I didn't hardly believe it!"

"It's a fact," Erskine answered.

"It sho' 'nuff is!" Studebaker jumped to his feet and began running back and forth, first one way then another.

"Now don't you worry yourself none, Mr. Erskine," he called out as he ran hither and yon, like a chicken with its head cut off. "We gonna have you outa that hole in a minute. Let's see what I can find. Gotta have somethin'. Gotta have somethin'. Musky-dime vines? Not strong enough. Tree limb? Ain't got nothin' to cut it with. Saplins? Too flimsy, not long enough."

He stopped suddenly, threw both hands in the air, and exclaimed, "Thank you, Lord. Thank you, Lord." With that, he turned and rushed back to peer down into the hole.

"Mr. Erskine, you wearin' a belt?"

"A belt? Why, yes I am," Erskine answered.

"Willie T. Nock, you wearin' a belt?" Studebaker asked, and Willie T.'s eyes lit up as he answered yes, he was wearing a belt.

"I got one too," Studebaker told us. "Mr. Erskine, toss your belt up here. Um hmm! You're a lucky man today, all us menfolks got belts."

He fastened the three leather belts together, wrapped one end tight around his right hand, and dropped the other end down into the dark hole. Lying flat on his stomach with his head and one arm over the edge of the pit, he instructed me and my cousin to grab onto his feet and hang on for dear life.

"Y'all two hold onto my feets, now. I don't look to fall in there my own self, and end up trapped in no hole with no white-cracker school teacher.

"Excuse me, Mr. Erskine," he added respectfully. "But that's sure enough the truth! You grab hold, now."

Erskine grabbed ahold and Studebaker held on tight with both hands and, just like that, hauled our teacher out of the hole. Witch Boy let loose a long, jubilant howl as Erskine Batson appeared out of the depths and scrambled to safety over the weedy ground.

We were all purely overcome with joy. And Erskine was pleased as punch to be rescued out of the hole before midnight-thirty, no doubt about it. After about a minute of the two men shaking hands and patting each other on the back, Studebaker returned their belts to Erskine and Willie T., and we all agreed that it was time for us to head for home as fast as we could.

"I surely do appreciate it! I just can't thank you enough," Erskine repeated, shaking Studebaker Freeman's hand one more time as we started down the dark road toward home. "I'm in your debt, pure and simple! Anything I can ever do to repay the favor, you just say the word!"

"You got any Co-Colas?" Studebaker inquired.

It was with a good deal of relief that we all arrived back at my house, the autumn night pitch black around us and the autumn wind tossing and heaving us to and fro. I was sure glad to see the soft glow of the light through the kitchen window as we climbed the back porch steps, still in various degrees of alarm and dishevelment.

"There!" I heard my daddy call out as we stomped across the porch.

"There they are," Mama announced. Then, as she watched me and Willie T., Studebaker Freeman, Erskine Batson, and Witch Boy file into the small crowded kitchen, she added, "Y'all stayed out too long."

Aunt Rachel and Uncle Buddy Nock were sitting at the kitchen table, and I saw Aunt Rachel eyeballing Studebaker first, then Erskine with a skeptical gaze. Daddy started pushing seats around and pulled a couple of extra cane-bottom chairs up to the table.

"Here, y'all have a seat, everybody. Just in time for supper!"

He reached over the table and shook Erskine's hand. "Good to see you, Erskine," he said. Then he shook Studebaker's hand. "Good to see you, Stu. Y'all *all* been out trick-or-treating?"

Erskine cleared his throat as he took a seat. "Somethin' like that. We — uh — brought the scholars home," he offered as an explanation.

"We appreciate that," Mama said, giving me and Willie T. a suspicious eye.

"Good evening, Miss Nash, Mr. Nash, Miss Nock, Mr. Nock," Studebaker greeted each person seated at the table. He sat down beside Erskine, then raised his eyebrows and scrutinized the table cloth in front of him.

Mama hopped up, grabbed two extra plates out of the kitchen cabinet, and placed one in front of each of the two unexpected guests. Aunt Rachel rolled her eyes and Uncle Buddy Nock grinned.

Erskine pulled our crumpled trick-or-treat bags out of his coat pockets and placed them on the table beside the fried pork chops, turnip greens, and cornbread. We quickly bowed our heads as my daddy offered a hasty blessing.

"Lord, we thank you for the many blessings we receive today."

"Um hm, that's sure enough the truth," Studebaker exclaimed. "Thank you, Jesus."

The wind howled outside, all through the dark woods and around our little house that evening as we sat around the kitchen table, safe and sound, happy and whole. That Halloween night was a night I'd remember, no doubt about it. It almost makes my heart stop beating to think about how close we came to a real disaster, me and Willie T. and Erskine. I knew we owed Studebaker, our rescuer, a world of thanks for getting Erskine out of that hole. But I had no way in the world of knowing that Erskine Batson's adventures on Moor's Gap Road had just begun.

Nine

The Maid of the Mist

Right after Halloween was over, the first thing Erskine did was to enlist the aid of his brother-in-law, Cowboy Howard, and his rescuer, Studebaker Freeman, and together the three of them filled up the pit he had chanced to discover out near Moor's Gap. The way the story goes, Erskine did a good deal of cussin' during this endeavor, and it's possible he may have dumped several loads of garbage from his garbage truck into the accursed hole. They also threw in a lot of the old stones and broken bricks from the crumbled walls of the stage coach inn, then covered it over with dirt and planted a little cherry laurel bush right on top of it all.

As soon as Willie T. heard about what they had done, he informed Erskine, in a round-about way, that he knew of another dangerous hole that just anybody could fall into if they happened to be meandering around Moonlight Ridge in the dark. He led the three men to the old church yard out in the woods, and helped them fill up the old empty well with fallen logs, rocks, and dirt. Afterwards he told me that, sure enough, there was no church there at all: just a big empty yard and a few scattered rocks and rotted boards. A few months earlier on a stormy summer night, me and Willie T., along with Henry Hope and Baby Junior Howard, had all taken cover in that old church building, only to find out afterward that there was no church there at all. I guess it just goes to show you.

After he made sure we were not in danger of killing ourselves by falling into gaping holes in the ground, our teacher started spending more and more time hanging around the old ruins of the stage coach inn. That suited me and Willie T. just fine because, as long as the weather held, we had decided to spend every second of free time out on Moor's Gap Road, transforming the mass of weeds, vines, and tumbled down stone walls into our own secret club house. We pretty much realized right from the beginning that we weren't going to be able to keep it a secret from Erskine, so we were happy to have his help, pulling weeds and shoveling dirt. As the long weeks of November passed, we were blessed by clear cold weather and the not-too-distant prospect of a week-long Thanksgiving break from school.

As soon as we got home from school every afternoon, we high-tailed it out in the woods and down to the old inn. In no time at all we had cleared out one entire room, roofless and open to the sky, with a wide, flat cobblestone walkway out front, and we decided that was enough for our clubhouse. We left the rest of the site to Erskine, who spent hours on his knees in the dirt and weeds, digging with a little bitty trowel, meticulously brushing dirt with a flat paint brush, sifting with a wire colander he'd stole from his mama's kitchen.

The strange thing about it was that right away we noticed things wouldn't stay where we left them. We collected a variety of odds and ends for furnishings: one wooden chair with no legs, a washtub that we turned upside down for a table, an old iron fireplace grate with an interesting design, and a few empty pickle jars without lids. Somehow it seemed like when our backs were turned, all these items had a life of their own. No matter how we arranged things, when we got back the next day, everything was scattered around all over the place. We wondered who was messing with our secret clubhouse, but Erskine said he figured it was probably raccoons and possums, tumbling things around looking for something to eat.

So we started bringing handfuls of Jim Dandy Dog Ration with us to scatter around, just in case, and that lured a bunch of big noisy crows out of the trees, trying to grab a peck or two away from Witch Boy, whenever they saw a chance.

With the crows and the dog eating up everything as fast as we put it out, we realized our strategy wasn't working, and meanwhile all our clubhouse goods still kept being moved around every time we turned our backs. Each time we arrived, we'd find the washtub rolled into a corner, the legless chair across on the other side of the room, and the pickle jars filled with dead leaves and spiny sweet-gum balls.

"That is somewhat suspicious," Erskine told us as he emptied the jars full of leaves and sweet-gum balls. "Somebody's foolin' around, looks like. Could'a been a raccoon, I guess. But more than likely a person, to move that washtub around like that."

He scanned the woods around us. It was the middle of November and the air was cold and crisp and clear. Trees as tall as the sky dropped yellow and brown leaves on us every time the wind blew. "I'd say, just to be on the safe side, y'all don't need to be out here by yourself, anyway. Till we discover who we're dealing with."

Willie T. and I just looked at each other. A bunch of enormous black crows circled above us, then lit in a nearby pine tree, cawing insistently, like they were trying to warn us about something.

Erskine set the glass jars down on the wooden seat of the legless chair, and wandered past his latest dig, off into the woods. Willie T. and I were busy rearranging things the way we wanted them to be, so we didn't ask him where he was going. But Witch Boy followed him.

The crows stopped their raucous cawing and everything was awfully quiet. Willie T. squatted down and started poking at something wedged between two cobble stones.

"Lookee here," he announced, holding up what I thought looked like a small clump of mud. "It's a earbob!"

Sure enough, when he used his shirt tail to wipe away the crust of dried mud, there was a beautiful earring made of rubies or red glass, sparkling in the palm of his hand.

"Let me see!" I gasped, reaching for the treasure. "Erskine's gonna have a fit!"

Willie T. held the earbob up and shook it playfully. There was a little circle of tiny red stones at the top, with a big dark red teardrop shaped jewel dangling down underneath.

"Purty," my cousin declared. He dropped the earring into my hand, then started scuffing his feet on the stone floor and prodding around with a stick. "Wonder if the other one's around here somewheres."

The ruby earring was beautiful, with a fancy border of gold surrounding each of the perfect red stones.

"Filigree," I said, remembering that I had heard Mawmaw say something like that before. "Filigree," I repeated.

"Filly what?" Willie T. asked. "Sounds like some kind of a Cajun word."

"No, not filly," I told him. "Filigree. It's the gold design around the red rubies. I've heard Mawmaw telling one of her tales, about somebody a long time ago, a beautiful woman who wore fancy earbobs made out of rubies and gold filigree."

Willie T. shrugged. "Reckon who it was?"

Then after a few seconds he continued. "You know what? I wonder who it was that pulled me up outa that hole the other day...on Halloween? I felt somebody grab ahold of my arm and yank me outta that hole. I couldn't hardly reach far enough to get a good grip and pull myself out. But it felt like somebody pulled me out."

"But didn't you see anybody when you got out?" I asked.

"There wasn't nobody to be seen," he answered with a shrug of his shoulders.

I dropped the beautiful earring into the pocket of my coat and started helping Willie T. search the ground.

"I wish we could find the —"

I stopped short and peered at my cousin who was staring back at me with his eyeballs as big as goose eggs.

"Listen," he whispered.

"Did you hear somebody laughing?" I asked.

"Yeah, I did," he answered, looking off into the woods. "It must have been Erskine, maybe."

But it hadn't sounded like Erskine. It sounded like a girl.

"Mr. Erskine!" Willie T. called.

No answer.

"Erskine Batson?" my cousin yelled again.

We both stood stock still, our eyes fixed on the woods where Erskine had disappeared earlier. Willie T. put his hands on his hips and snorted.

"Now where's he gone off to?"

"Call of nature, maybe," I suggested.

"May be," my cousin mumbled skeptically. But neither of us moved.

"Come on," Willie T. grunted impatiently. "Let's go find him. I'm gettin' hungry and I'm ready to go home." He whistled sharply and called for Witch Boy.

"Here, Witch Boy! Come on, boy!"

We heard the dog barking gleefully in the distance, right before he came bounding out of the woods.

"There you are!" I greeted the dog as he danced around us, wagging his long tail as hard as he could. "Now, where's Mr. Erskine?"

Witch Boy, too smart for his own good, tore out running back into the woods to find Erskine. Willie T. and I agreed we might as well follow him.

Out on the mountain, people have seen a lot of strange things that can't be explained. When my Granny Rilla was just a little girl, she saw a perfect little woman, no taller than your hand, splashing in the Grind Rock Spring. My daddy saw the wolfeener, a terrible scary beast with a big head and long sharp teeth, when it turned on his hunting dogs, grabbing them up in its mouth and throwing them through the air. And everybody in the family had seen that dipper in the water bucket at Mawmaw's house, spinning around and around until somebody got up enough courage to grab it and lay it on the shelf beside the bucket. That always happens just the same, every single night, if nobody remembers to take the dipper out of the bucket before going to bed.

My mother saw a black panther up in a tree when she was walking up the mountain one evening, and it jumped down and landed on the dirt road right behind her, scaring her so bad she ran out of her shoes and ran all the way home barefooted. And we'd heard Papa Jasper telling about the horrible loup-garou that chased the preacher into the thicket and stole his straw hat.

So, with all that in mind, Willie T. and I more or less took it in stride when we walked through the bushes and saw the ghost girl.

But Erskine Batson? He looked like he was about to faint and fall back in it.

Just as we pushed our way out of the bushes, we saw what first appeared to be a patch of fog, or smoke, something white moving through the trees toward our teacher. I blinked my eyes, and a dark skinned girl stepped toward us out of the fog. She had dark brown skin and black hair hanging in a long braid over her shoulder.

Erskine looked over at me as I raised my hand and silently pointed at the girl.

"I see her," he whispered. And quick as a flash, she disappeared.

"What the Sam Hill was that?" Willie T. blurted out. I had to declare that I had no way in the world of knowing.

I glanced at Erskine, who was looking none too steady on his feet.

"Erskine?" I murmured.

"I ... I saw her," the suddenly pale teacher replied, waving his hand toward the trees. "All up there under those trees, she sort of comes and goes ... like smoke. And I heard her laugh."

"We heard that, too," Willie T. said as he stepped closer to Erskine and touched his sleeve. Erskine swayed.

"Are you fixin' to fall down?" my cousin asked him. "Breathe, Mr. Erskine ..."

"What?"

"You're not breathin'. Get your breath, before you —"

Erskine gasped, then sat right down on the ground in the leaves and the dirt, his arms on his knees.

"Are you all right?" Willie T. and I both asked at the same time.

"Whew! I can't say that I'm all right," he stammered, shaking his head.

Then he laughed. "Look, Halloween is over with. Are y'all two playin' tricks on me, now?"

"Nah," Willie T. answered softly. "We didn't have a thang to do with it."

"Look!" I whispered. "She's back."

And sure enough, there she stood right before us, almost close enough to touch. And she was beautiful. She wore a long black skirt and a ruffled cotton blouse with a long black shawl over it. Her black hair was tied with a red ribbon. And she wore one red earring.

"Who are you?" Erskine breathed, sounding like he couldn't find his voice.

There wasn't a sound, except the wind rustling through the dry autumn leaves.

"Are you Bess?" Erskine whispered.

Then the expression on her face changed and suddenly she looked terribly sad. She turned her face away from us, then right before our eyes, she stepped back into the bushes and completely disappeared.

"I, God!" Erskine gasped. "Was it Bess?"

"Bess? Bess who?" Willie T. asked.

"Bess, the landlord's daughter," Erskine answered.

"Well, who's that?" Willie T. demanded.

Erskine just shook his head. He stood up and brushed the leaves and dirt off the back of his coat.

"Let's us go home," he said.

Ten

An Old Legend

The three of us came down Moor's Gap Road that evening without looking back. The whole scary affair, however, hadn't affected Witch Boy one little bit, and he danced and bounced along beside us, happy as a lark, as we trudged silently down the rocky dirt road toward familiar territory.

It was Friday night, so we didn't have to worry about going to school the next day, and Willie T. was spending the night at my house, as usual. Our teacher was still looking fairly peaked in the face, and I expected him to head on home. But when we came over the rise where Mawmaw's house sat, he hesitated. Staring at the dark little wooden house, he ran his fingers through his hair and let out a long noisy sigh.

"I believe I'll go in and talk to Uncle Jasper," he told us. "Y'all get on home, now."

"Gyaah!" Willie T. complained. "That ain't fair!"

Erskine eyed my cousin. "Don't your mama and daddy *ever* expect you to come home?"

"Not tonight!" Willie T. exclaimed. "I'm spendin' the night at Aunt Sara and Uncle Sam's house. Mama and Daddy's gone to the picture show to see *The Creature With the Atom Brain!*"

Erskine sighed.

"No arguin' with that," he conceded, raising his hands in the air. I believe it was because of the shock he'd just been through that made him give up so easy.

"I'll run down the hill and tell Mama and Daddy where we are," I volunteered. "Be right back."

The two of them walked slowly up the front porch steps as Witch Boy and I took off down the hill.

If you're standing in Mawmaw's front yard, you can look down and see my house just a little ways down the hill. So it only took a minute for me to run in and out again. I took time to hug Daddy's neck in the living room where he was reading the newspaper, give Mama a brief explanation in the kitchen where she was putterin' around at the stove, and then scoot back out the front door with Witch Boy at my heels.

"Hurry back," Mama called after us. "Supper'll get cold."

"Mama's got supper on the table," I announced as soon as I charged through the front door, back at Mawmaw's house. Papa looked interested.

Erskine stood in the middle of the room, shifting from one foot to the other while Willie T., eyebrows akimbo, gazed up at him.

Mawmaw looked impatient.

"Jasper, I believe the boy's got somethin' he wants to say," she informed Papa. "Y'all set down here. I've got coffee on the stove, anybody wants some."

We all sat down around the kitchen table with a kerosene lamp in the middle of the red and white checked oil cloth. The kerosene lamp gave off a warm bright glow without lighting the dark corners of the room. Witch Boy sat on the floor and put his head in my lap, and thumped the linoleum with his long old tail. Willie T. and I stared at each other. Erskine cleared his throat nervously as Mawmaw set the coffee cups in front of each of us. She put a big cream pitcher full of sweet milk in front of me and Willie T., and I knew she expected us to fill our cups nearly full of milk, then she'd add just a dab of coffee. She pushed the cut glass bowl of honey toward us, and we obediently plopped a couple of big spoonfuls into our cups as she poured steaming, fragrant coffee from a beat-up tin coffee pot.

"Thank you, ma'am," Erskine finally spoke, raising an eyebrow as he stared at the bowl of honey. "Aunt Laurie, if you've got any long sweetenin', I'd be much obliged."

"Why, sure I do, Erskine. I got molasses," Mawmaw answered, and she brought a big jar of dark brown syrup to the table.

"No bee juice for me," Erskine announced with a smile as he poured a generous amount of sticky sweet molasses into his cup.

Willie T. and I stirred and waited. Erskine sipped his hot coffee and appeared to finally relax a little.

"Uncle Jasper, I was wonderin' if you could sing me that song again, about the highwayman? And the landlord's daughter? I tried to sing a little of that song to my two scholars here, a couple of days ago," Erskine continued. "But all I could remember of it was the end ..."

Pausing, he shifted in his chair, then chuckled softly.

"Then we got somewhat distracted by other concerns."

"Law, if you keep on messin' around that old stage coach stop..." Mawmaw eyed Erskine Batson like a judge in a courtroom starin' at the guilty party. "Most folks around here have enough sense to stay away from that place."

Willie T. and I automatically focused our gaze on our coffee cups. Willie T. began humming tunelessly and wiggled around on his seat, causing the cane bottom chair to creak and squawk like a speckled guinea hen.

Papa set his coffee cup down and leaned both arms on the table, gazing at Erskine for a few seconds before he spoke.

"Seems like I remember everybody around here used to sing that highwayman song, back when I was a boy. I reckon I can sing it again for you. But, Laurie's right. You'd all be better off to stay away from that place. No good can come of it. Stir things up that's best left alone. See somethin' you don't need to see. Some things you don't want to mess with."

"Well, yes sir," Erskine replied. "You're most likely right about that."

Papa stood and pulled his chair back from the table, and retrieved his guitar out of a dark corner of the room. "You say your mama has supper on the table?" he asked as he sat down, holding the old guitar.

I nodded my head, and Willie T. swung his legs back and forth a few times, looking impatient.

"It's a melancholy song for these younguns to be listening to," Mawmaw said.

Papa plucked a few strings and twisted a tuning peg or two. Then, in his soft deep voice that sounded so much like my daddy's voice, he sang the old song about the ill-fated highwayman and Bess, the landlord's beautiful black haired daughter.

The Highwayman

The wind was a torrent of darkness among the gusty trees.
The moon was a ghostly galleon, tossed upon cloudy seas.
And the road was a ribbon of moonlight
over the purple moor.
And the highwayman came riding, riding, riding.
Yes, the highwayman came riding up to the old inn door.

Over the cobbles he clattered
and clashed in the dark inn-yard.
And he tapped with his whip on the window,
but all was locked and barred.
So he whistled a tune to the window,
and who should be waiting there,
but the landlord's black-eyed daughter,
Bess the landlord's daughter,
plaiting a dark red love knot into her long black hair.

"One kiss my bonny sweetheart
for I'm after a prize tonight.
But I shall be back with the yellow gold
before the morning light.
Yet if they press me sharply and harry me through the day
then, look for me by moonlight,
watch for me by moonlight,
and I'll come to thee by moonlight,
though hell should bar the way."

He did not come at the dawning,
 he did not come at the noon.
And out of the tawny sunset, before the rise of the moon,
when the road was a gypsy's ribbon
looping the purple moor,
Oh, a Redcoat troop came marching, marching, marching.
King George's men came marching up to the old inn door.

And they bound the landlord's daughter
with many a sniggering jest,
and they bound the musket beside her
with the barrel beneath her breast.
"Now, keep good watch," and they kissed her.
She heard the doomed man say,
"Oh, look for me by moonlight,
watch for me by moonlight,
and I'll come to thee by moonlight,
though hell should bar the way."

"Look for me by moonlight." Hoof beats ringing clear.
"Watch for me by moonlight."
Were they deaf, that they did not hear?
For he rode on the gypsy highway,
she breathed one final breath.
Then her finger moved in the moonlight,

her musket shattered the moonlight,
and it shattered her breast in the moonlight
and warned him with her death.

He turned, he spurred on to the west.
He did not know who stood
bound with her black hair a'flowin' down,
drenched with her own red blood.
No, not till the dawn had he heard it,
and his face grew gray to hear
how Bess, the Landlord's daughter,
the landlord's black eyed daughter,
had watched for her love in the moonlight,
and died in the darkness there.

Back he spurred, like a madman,
shrieking a curse to the sky,
with the white road smoking behind him,
and his rapier brandished high.
Blood red were his spurs in the golden moon,
wine red his velvet coat,
when they shot him down on the highway,
down like a dog on the highway,
and he lay in his blood on the highway
with a bunch of lace at his throat.

And still, of a winter's night, they say,
when the wind is in the trees
and the moon is a ghostly galleon tossed upon cloudy seas,
when the road is a ribbon of moonlight,
loopin' the purple moor,
oh, the highwayman comes riding, riding, riding.
Yes, the highwayman comes riding, up to the old inn door.

We all sat quiet after the song was over. I listened to the clock on the fireplace mantel, ticking, ticking, in the otherwise silent room. Mawmaw sat looking down at her hands in her lap, like she was thinking about something, and Papa stared down at the old guitar in his hands like he suddenly didn't recognize it and wondered how it ended up in his hands.

Erskine's eyes were closed and his head was tilted back a little, and I thought he might possibly have gone to sleep.

Mawmaw Laurie was right. The song was too sad for me and Willie T. I tried to keep my breath from coming out in sobs, but I failed in that futile attempt. Willie T. sat holding the edge of his chair in a death grip, his eyebrows raised up nearly to the top of his head.

"Poor ol' Loo Pin!" he moaned softly, barely above a whisper. "Sounds like a Chinese to me. And . . . why was he purple?"

Erskine Batson opened his eyes and shook his head. He looked like somebody trying to figure out a puzzle, with his lips pressed tight together and his eyebrows squinched in a knot.

"Willie T. Nock, what the Sam Hill are you talking about now?" he asked in a soft, deep voice, like somebody coming out of a sound sleep.

Willie T.'s trick knee took the initiative. His leg jerked spasmodically, and it looked like he may have intended to kick the leg of my chair, but instead his foot connected with the near-hypnotized Witch Boy's rump, and the ensuing ruckus broke the quiet spell that had overcome us all.

"Lord, Lord!" Mawmaw exclaimed as we all jumped up in a seizure of panic.

"Uncle Jasper said it in the song!" Willie T. yelped as he hopped around, trying to avoid stepping on the bouncing, barking dog. "You told us a Moor was a colored man, and Uncle Jasper just now said 'Loo Pin, the purple Moor!' "

Erskine sighed and wiped one hand across his eyes. "It's not the same word, Willie T. A totally different concept, entirely. The road in the moonlight was 'looping the purple moor.' It's like a wide field that looks purple in the moonlight. Not a purple *human* Moor."

"Humph," Papa grunted. He returned his suddenly recognizable old guitar to its place in the dark corner, grabbed his gray fedora off the nail by the fireplace, then gazed at Erskine who was preoccupied with scratching his head and stretching his long arms in various peculiar exercises.

"But you said —" Willie T. began, but Erskine cut in.

"This might take some explainin'. It's called a homonym."

"A what? Hominy?" the totally confused Willie T. exclaimed.

"Homo-nym," Erskine slowly repeated. "Two or more words having the same spelling but different meanings."

All eyes, including the dog's, were on our teacher.

"We'll take it up, in the classroom," he said finally.

"Humph," Papa grunted again, adjusting his hat securely on his head. "Let's go see what Sara has on the table. Maybe she'll have some hominy." He opened the front door and a strong cold wind blasted into the room. "Grab your coat, Laurie," he instructed over the howl of the wind. "Cold out here."

Mawmaw slipped on her heavy wool coat, a nubby tweed affair that hung from her shoulders to the floor, and she hastily tied a three-cornered scarf around her head. She cupped her hand and, with a loud puff, blew out the flame of kerosene lamp, then we all filed out the front door, leaving the dark little room empty behind us.

A full moon hung big and round and white behind the immense black pine trees towering above us. As we hastily made our way down the hill, we heard Bu, the hoot owl, calling from somewhere out in the woods, and Willie T., forgetting the hominy and the homonyms, called back, imitating the ancient owl.

"Who, who, who are you? Who, who, I'm out here too."

Eleven

The Crow

I woke up in the middle of the night to the sound of something tapping on my bedroom window. I lay still for a minute or two, half in and half out of sleep in the moonlit room, listening to the sharp tap, tap, tap on the window pane.

My first thought was that Willie T. must be up, must be outside, tapping on my window trying to wake me up. But there was enough light from the moon that I could clearly see straight from my bedroom into the living room where my cousin lay sound asleep on the devonette, tangled in a mess of quilts, sheets, and brown dog.

The house was still and silent.

It was cold in my bedroom. I sat up and peered at the window near the foot of my bed. I didn't much want to get out from under my warm quilt, and I sure didn't want to know what in the world was tapping at my window. I just wanted it to stop.

Tap, tap, tap. Tap, tap, tap.

With an awful feeling of dread, I wondered if the loup-garou ever tapped on your window to trick you into letting him in so he could grab you and say, "I got you now, me." I had a horrible feeling that it was a possibility. I looked at Willie T. and Witch Boy, dead to the world on the devonette

86

in the living room just a few feet away, and wondered if I ought to wake them up. Then I remembered how Mawmaw always said it's best to let sleeping dogs lie.

Tap, tap, tap. Tap, tap, tap.

I focused my sleepy eyes on the window, and there was enough moonlight coming in that I could see a dark shape against my yellow gingham curtains. It looked pretty big, but not as big as a person. Not as big as the loup-garou. Not as big as the wolfeener.

"Maybe it's just a possum," I said out loud, and I opened the curtain.

It was a huge black crow.

When I pulled the curtain back, the crow stopped tapping and leaned closer to the window, turning his black head first one way then another, peering at me through the window pane. His round black eyes glittered in the moonlight.

As I leaned closer to get a better look at him, he chose that precise moment to attack the window pane again, making such a loud racket I almost jumped out of my skin.

I yanked the curtain back and raised the window with the idea of trying to scare the noisy crow away. That's not what the crow had in mind, however. Quicker than you could say Jack Robinson, he was in my room, pretty much making himself at home.

Earlier that night, before getting into bed, I had emptied my coat pockets of the day's various treasures, leaving it all scattered on my dresser. Hickory nuts, unusual-looking rocks, some crusty chipped marbles, and the perfectly beautiful ruby-red earbob, were all piled on top of my wadded up handkerchief, white batiste with lace on one corner.

The enormous crow perched on the footboard of my bed, looked left and right, then hopped onto the dresser, awkwardly stomping around in the pile of hickory nuts, rocks, and marbles. He got one of his long toes caught in the delicate lace edging of my white handkerchief, and he raised his foot to his beak and pecked peevishly. I didn't have any idea what you're supposed to do if your bedroom gets invaded by a crow in the middle of the night, so I just watched. And wouldn't you know it, he left off pecking at the handkerchief and went straight for the beautiful ruby-red earbob.

He picked it up in his big black beak, dropped it back onto the dresser, then picked it up again, like he was examining it. Then the crow in the mirror suddenly caught his beady-eyed attention. He dropped the shiny piece of jewelry and carefully poked it under a hickory nut, then gave the mirror a loud experimental whack.

I guess old mister crow had never seen a mirror before in his life, and he didn't expect the other crow to attack with no warning whatsoever. It looked to me like the sudden movement of his own reflection just about gave the bird a heart attack. He lurched backwards, flapping his huge black wings, emitting a loud nerve-shattering caw, and noisily scattering the pile of treasures in every direction.

That's when Witch Boy woke up.

It's hard to say what all happened next, but it all happened awfully fast. Witch Boy was all over the room, leaping, snapping, and barking everywhere at once. Mister Crow, dangling my favorite handkerchief from one long toe, flew and flapped first one direction then another, landed back on the dresser, then attacked his reflection with amazing zeal. The crazy dog tried to leap onto the dresser but lost his balance. Dog, bird, hickory nuts, rocks, and marbles hit the hard wooden floor with a clattering crash.

"Caw!" the bird screamed as he watched the hickory nuts and rocks and marbles rolling in every direction across the floor. Holding the ruby earring firmly in his huge beak and trailing my white handkerchief from his right foot, the crow more or less circled the room with the crazy brown dog in hot pursuit.

Right in the middle of this horrible melee, Willie T. appeared in my doorway just moments before my mama rushed in, barefooted on the cold floor and dressed in her typical nighttime attire of a white cotton petticoat and an old raggedy flannel shirt.

Willie T. yelled "What the Sam Hill?" and started to chase the dog, but quickly jumped out of the way as bird and dog headed straight for him.

"What in the world are you doing?" mama cried, obviously blaming me for the entire affair. Then she crouched and threw her hands in the air and let out a piercing shriek as the giant crow, still dangling my white handkerchief from his ridiculous toe, tried to land on her head.

Mama ducked, Willie T. squatted, and I ran to the window, hoping that maybe the crow would decide to go back out the way he came in. I grabbed hold of the curtain with the idea that I would hold it out of the way so the frantic crow could see the open window, but in my state of panic, I jerked too hard and the curtain and curtain rod clattered to the floor with a crash. Not one to pass up such a fine opportunity, Witch Boy wasted no time getting tangled in the yellow checked curtains, and continued his mad chase, dragging curtains and curtain rod behind him.

I stood at the open window, waving my arms and gesturing like a traffic cop and yelling as loud as I possibly could.

"Out! Out! Get out! Go this way! Get out!"

Following my instructions more or less to a tee, after once again attempting to land on my mama's head as she crouched amid the hickory nuts, rocks, and marbles on my floor, the crow sailed out the window, taking the ruby earbob and my white handkerchief with him.

Willie T. raced to the window and got a choke hold on Witch Boy, who was attempting to leap out the window but couldn't make it, being totally and completely encumbered by my yellow curtains and the metal curtain rod.

"Was that a damn bird, or what?" Willie T. screeched, sticking his head out the window while wrestling Witch Boy into submission.

"A damn bird!" mama hollered, in a very surprising burst of profanity. She stumbled over some of the various items on the floor, held her hands out to catch her balance, and gazed around my destroyed bedroom. "A damn bird!" she repeated.

My daddy chose this moment to appear in the doorway. He turned on the bright overhead light, blinding us all, and stood there in his orange plaid cotton boxer shorts, surveying the destruction of my bedroom.

"They! Why have y'all got the winder open?" he asked. "It's cold in here."

Mama shielded her eyes with both hands and stared at Daddy.

"It was a dang great-big black bird!" Willie T. declared, pointing out the window into the chilly darkness.

Daddy raised his eyebrows and slowly scanned the messy room. His sleepy gaze came to rest on Witch Boy, sporting yellow curtains, panting and wagging his tail briskly through the air, back and forth, back and forth. Daddy shook his head, looking disappointed with the whole bunch of us.

"Well, don't y'all reckon it's about time to get in the bed?" he asked wearily.

We all nodded our heads and mumbled that we agreed it was just about that time.

I retrieved my curtains off of the dog, Mama and Daddy wandered back to their bedroom and, shivering with cold, I finally closed the window. Willie T. and Witch Boy ambled back into the living room and crawled under the covers on the devonette. I turned out the blinding overhead light and collapsed onto my bed. After taking one last look at the black night and the big white moon outside my bare window, I pulled the quilt over my head and fell asleep. All night long I dreamed that I was flying, chasing behind a giant black crow who carried a ruby red earbob and a white lace-trimmed handkerchief, sailing through the dark autumn sky.

Twelve

Evy and Midnight

The next morning after the crow episode, the house was quiet and peaceful, Daddy was out in the yard tinkering with the carburetor of his old black pick-up truck, and Mama was lurking in the kitchen, cooking bacon, scrambled eggs, and grits. She came to the doorway and took a critical look around my bedroom without saying a word, then escaped back into the safety of the kitchen.

Willie T. wandered in, barefooted and bleary eyed, and with his help my bedroom was soon in tolerable condition. He straightened out the disfigured metal curtain rod and helped me get the yellow curtains back on the window.

"I aint' never lettin' no dang crow in *my* bedroom," he announced when we had done all we could to restore my room to a normal state of affairs. "That bird was crazy!"

"He took the ruby earring," I said, trying to think of some word worse than 'crazy' to describe the crow.

"Do you thank that's what he came after?" Willie T. asked. "The earbob?"

The truth is, I hadn't thought of that possibility. But now that my cousin asked, I had to admit that the crow acted like he wanted in my room awfully bad, like he was looking for something in particular.

"Bur how do you reckon he could have known that I had the earbob in my bedroom?" I asked.

"I don't know," Willie T. replied. "Might a' seen us pick it up out there in the woods. Dang snoopy bird!"

"Breakfast is ready!" Mama called from the kitchen. The tantalizing smell of coffee and bacon drifted through the house.

Daddy came in, washed his hands in the dishpan, and the four of us sat down to a quiet, subdued breakfast. Daddy gave me and Willie T. a couple of suspicious looks, like he was trying to figure out which one of us was to blame for the previous night's ruckus. I was pretty sure that if anybody was to blame, it was me, so I kept my head down and concentrated on my scrambled eggs. It suddenly occurred to me that someone was missing.

"Where's Witch Boy?" I asked, sitting up straight and staring all around the kitchen.

"He's out yonder in the woods somewhere," Daddy replied. "He went out with me this morning and made a bee line up the hill into the woods. Gone huntin', I expect."

"Crazy dog," my cousin mumbled around a mouthful of biscuit.

"Um hmm," Daddy replied. "At least he wasn't wearin' a pair of yeller window curtains, though."

After breakfast was finished, Mama and Daddy announced that they were fixin' to go down to Aunt Rachel and Uncle Buddy Nock's house for a little while. Daddy said he wanted to see what he could find out about *The Creature With the Atom Brain*.

"I believe I might'a went to school with that feller," he told us. "Sara, you remember Brainy McCraney don't you?"

Mama glared at Daddy and snickered, but didn't answer.

As soon as my parents and the old black pickup were out of sight, Willie T. and I threw on our coats, grabbed a couple of soft crumbly left-over biscuits, and headed for Moor's Gap.

Overnight a light fog had settled over the mountain, and it lingered, gray and still, among the trees. Then, as we scampered along the dirt trail leading up and over the mountain, a brisk autumn wind swept through the red and gold trees, sweeping away the fog like a witch's broom sweeping away cobwebs, and low and behold, it was a beautiful autumn morning.

The air was bright and clear as we followed the narrow winding dirt road, still discussing the previous night's escapades of the big black crow. We heard Witch Boy barking somewhere in the thick woods ahead of us.

"Chasin' a rabbit, I bet you a dollar and a half," Willie T. put forth.

As we ran along Moor's Gap Road, laughing and spluttering biscuit crumbs, any leftover feelings of apprehension or fright from the night before disappeared into the bright autumn sky above us. I don't guess there's anything in the world that does a better job of calming the heebie-jeebies than philandering around out in the woods on a bright autumn morning.

The two of us arrived at our destination in high spirits and found our run-away dog waiting for us, perched up on the crumbling rock wall and wagging his keen tail like a maniac. I gave him what was left of my biscuit, which he swallowed without hesitation. Then he bounded off the wall and loped away into the woods, barking loud enough to wake the dead.

We busied ourselves clearing fallen leaves and pinecones out of the roofless room we had designated as our clubhouse. Enormous pine trees perfumed the crisp air with their fresh green scent as they swayed around us. A pair of gray bushy-tailed squirrels stopped chasing one another just long enough to give us the eyeball, then they dashed away chattering and complaining.

Willie T., no doubt inspired by what our teacher called the lush countryside, began singing in a strident voice.

In the pines, in the pines,
Where the sun never shines,
I'll shiver when the cold wind blows.
I asked my love
For the time of day,
And she throwed her watch away.

He grabbed a long heavy stick and began beating a one-two-three, one-two-three rhythm on the bottom of our upside-down washtub that we used as a table. The racket he made caused the chattering squirrels to fuss even louder as they skittered through the bright green pine boughs over our heads.

My love, my love,
What did I do wrong
To make you treat me so?
In the pines, in the pines,
Where the sun never shines,
I'll shiver when the cold wind blows.

That's when I noticed how the things laying on the washtub bounced up and down every time Willie T. whacked the tub with the stick he was holding. I watched hickory nuts, acorns, pine straw, and dirt bouncing around, along with something I didn't expect to see: my white handkerchief with lace on one corner, folded up as pretty as you please.

"Stop! Stop!" I shouted, interrupting Willie T.'s percussions. "Look! It's my handkerchief!"

Willie T. stopped banging.

"How did this get here?" I asked, unfolding the white square of cloth and holding it in front of his face. "It's my handkerchief that the crow carried off last night! It was caught on his old long toe when he flew away!"

"Well, I'll be dang," Willie T. replied. He looked all around like he expected the big crow to be lurking somewhere nearby. "He must'a dropped it here when he flew over."

I wasn't sure about that possibility.

"I don't see how he could have dropped it, perfectly folded up so neat."

Willie T. looked around again, cautiously peering at the woods all around us.

"Well, could'a been somebody else found it where the crow dropped it, and they folded it up and left it layin' here."

I folded and unfolded the handkerchief.

"Could be," Willie T. insisted.

Witch Boy's gleeful bark could be heard out in the woods, along with the sounds of someone laughing.

Willie T. stood up, dropping the stick out of his hand, and it landed with a hollow sounding thump on the wash tub. "Listen," he said. "Somebody's comin'."

Low and behold, it was our teacher, thrashin' through the bushes with a big grin on his face. He raised his eyebrows and gave the two of us a quick glance, then held his hand out toward the thick bushes, like he was waiting for someone to follow him.

"It's all right," he said in a soothing tone of voice. "It's just my scholars."

My mouth fell open and I felt like the wind had been knocked out of my lungs when I saw who stepped into the clearing to take Erskine Batson's hand. It was the beautiful dark girl, the ghost girl, best I knew, that we had seen coming and going in the foggy mist. She looked solid enough today, as natural as anyone you'd ever want to see, with her long black hair hanging down in a braid over her shoulder. And, she was wearing two glittering ruby earrings.

"What the tarnation?" Willie T. gasped slowly. "Who in the world is that?"

The girl smiled.

Erskine Batson beamed.

"This is Evy," he said.

"I thought you called her Bess, other day," I exclaimed.

"Well, it looks like I was mistaken," Erskine replied.

The dark skinned girl continued to smile.

"My name's Evergreen," she said. Her voice sounded like music. "Folks calls me Evy."

Willie T.'s face broke into a wide grin, and he stepped toward the strange girl with his hand stretched out like he was going to touch her to see if she was real. She laughed that same musical laugh we had heard before, and moved around behind Erskine, then watched us from behind his shoulder. Her huge brown eyes made me think of the calm, deep eyes of a deer.

Willie T. exhaled, shrugged his shoulders, and shifted his attention to our teacher.

Still grinning ear-to-ear like a possum, Erskine asked, "Y'all are out traipsin' around the countryside awfully early this mornin', aren't you?"

Willie T. spluttered. "Well, we ain't no earlier than *you* are, looks to me like!" he declared, raising his eyebrows up and flinging his arms out in a sweeping gesture. "And we ain't traipsin' around the countryside. We're traipsin' around in our clubhouse."

"It's Erskine's clubhouse, too," I reminded him, punching him on the shoulder just about as hard as I could.

"This here *my* place," the beautiful girl said, interrupting me and Willie T. before we could get into a real scuffle. "Always been . . . always be."

Willie T. and I just stood there gaping at the pretty brown girl with the soft sweet voice. It seemed to me like there was something spooky about her voice, like it cast some sort of a magic spell over us, the same way a sad pretty song might do. I don't know any way to describe it except to say I felt bewitched. At that very moment, the thought came into my head that we were all bewitched. Most especially our teacher!

Erskine looked like he was on cloud nine! He spread his arms out, palms up to the sky, like it was all fine and dandy as far as he was concerned.

Just then, our crazy brown dog came bounding out of the woods, and to my total amazement, he ran straight to the girl, Evy, and flopped on the ground at her feet. With another musical sounding laugh, she squatted down and put her hands on each side of the dog's head, raising his face to hers and staring right into his eyes. It looked like she whispered something to him, and he yipped happily then tore out running around us in a wild circle, kicking up leaves, dirt, and pine straw as he went.

The black haired girl hitched her skirt up to her knees and sat down on the old legless kitchen chair, looking as natural as anybody you'd see. I was a little surprised to see that she was barefooted, though. Willie T. and I went barefooted all summer long, but with the weather changing and turning colder, we had enough sense to wear our shoes and socks.

Erskine sat down on the low portion of the old rock wall, right beside Evy, so Willie T. and I sat down too, on the ground beside the metal washtub. We all watched the dog tearing around the clearing in a crazy display of glee. Finally, Willie T. and I both called at the same time.

"Witch Boy! Stop it!"

He stopped short and gave himself a good shake from head to tail, then plopped down beside me with his head in my lap.

"Good dog," I told him, and he closed his eyes.

Willie T. couldn't take his eyes off the pretty girl, whatever she was: ghost or human, one or the other.

"Do you live around here somewheres?" he asked.

The girl glanced at Erskine before she answered. "Nearby."

My inquisitive cousin didn't look completely satisfied with that answer. I couldn't take my eyes off the beautiful red earrings, glistening against the girl's black hair. I noticed that underneath the ruby earrings, there were ugly scars on both of her earlobes, and somehow that looked strange to me. And Erskine? He looked as pleased as punch. If my Mawmaw Laurie had been there, she would have said that he looked like the cat that swallowed the canary.

"Well, where's your folks?" Willie T. persisted, not one to be easily put off.

"Nearby," she repeated in a soft voice. Then she tipped her head slightly toward the woods and added, "Over on Cat Bluff."

Willie T., frowning in the bright sunlight, followed her gaze up the side of the wooded hill.

"Gyaah!" he exclaimed. "Up there with the panthers and the bob cats, and whatever and all? I didn't know nobody lived up there! Aunt Sara seen a black panther jump down out of a tree behind her one time, didn't she, Lily Claire?"

I nodded my head.

"Like to scared her to death! You ever seen a panther?" he asked, narrowing his eyes at the strange young woman.

"I seen plenty," she answered. Erskine raised an eyebrow. The girl continued. "They ain't bother us none. We ain't bother them."

She sat up straight and fixed her gaze toward the woods, up the side of the hill. We all stared in that direction, and I couldn't hardly believe my eyes when a huge black crow came sailing out of the trees, headed straight for us. That bird looked awfully familiar to me. His huge wings grazed the top of my head and without thinking, I threw my arms up to cover my face.

The girl laughed, disregarding me and Willie T. as we jumped up and scrambled out of the way.

"Thar he," she announced. "This here be Midnight." And the big black crow landed, easy as you please, on her shoulder.

"It's that dang bird!" Willie T. exclaimed over the noise of Witch Boy's excited barking.

"Tell these folkses hello, Midnight," the girl crooned, shifting her shoulder and making the crow dance and ruffle his feathers. The crow didn't tell us hello, he just gave us a dirty look and bobbed his head up and down a few times.

Erskine, meanwhile, laughed out loud, looking as amused as a fool at the circus.

I watched with my eyeballs out on stems as the crow nuzzled his enormous black beak against the girl's cheek, then turning his beady eyes on the red jewel dangling from her ear, he pecked at it industriously. She smiled and spoke to the bird in some language I didn't understand. Witch Boy was having a fit, and I wrapped my arms around his neck, hanging on best I could.

"You can let that ol' dog go," the girl told me, holding her hand out toward me and the leaping, yelping dog. "These two is friends."

Clinging to the writhing, wiggling, dog, I stared at the girl, thinking that didn't sound like a good idea to me. Then I turned loose.

Witch Boy shot out of my arms and leaped onto Evy's lap. She didn't pay the leggy, lanky dog any more mind than if he'd been a tiny puppy, and she wrapped one arm around his neck and nuzzled her face into his brown fur. The big old crow pecked mischievously at the top of Witch Boy's brown head, and the dog rolled on his back and lay on the girl's lap, kicking his four long legs in a spasm of delight.

Erskine reached over and rubbed Witch Boy's lean belly.

"So, it looks like y'all know each other, then," he said.

"We knows each other," she replied. She looked straight at Erskine, then at Willie T., and then at me. "I knows all of you."

Something about the way she said that sent a shiver down my spine, and Willie T. caught his breath in a noisy gasp.

"Gyah! It was *you* that pulled me out of that hole! You're the one, ain't you? I seen you!"

Jumping to his feet, he slapped both hands against his pants legs in a gesture of surprise. Erskine and I both stared at the girl, waiting for an answer.

But before anyone could say anything else, a sudden strong wind caught us all off guard, swirling pine straw and fallen leaves up into a perfect whirlwind around us. The big crow shrieked one raspy caw and flew off into the woods. We all stood up, shielding our eyes against the whirling dust and grit. I closed my eyes and when I opened them a second later, the girl was nowhere in sight.

Erskine raised his arms, trying to protect his face and eyes from the onslaught of wind and leaves, and looked first one way then another, searching for where the girl had disappeared to.

"Well, let's us go back down the mountain," he shouted, pushing me and Willie T. ahead of him as we picked our way down the dirt trail.

Thirteen

The Rapture

The wind didn't let up, and we were all nearly choked to death by flying dust by the time we made it down Moor's Gap Road. Witch Boy snorted and shook his head as we ran up the front porch steps at my house.

Erskine stopped briefly on the front porch, holding one lapel of his heavy black coat against his face.

"Y'all okay?" he yelled.

We nodded and yelled that we were pretty much all right.

"Then I'm headed home. Get inside out of this blasted wind!" And he loped off the porch and disappeared into the storm.

Me and Willie T. and Witch Boy dashed into the shelter of the quiet house. Together, Willie T. and I both heaved the door shut against the violent wind.

"Gyaah!" my cousin exclaimed. "I ain't never —"

"Me neither," I agreed.

The dog snorted and raked a front paw over his dust-caked nose a couple of times.

"What kind of a dang wind was that?" Willie T. inquired, pulling off his coat and giving it a rambunctious shake. "And where'd that girl run off to so fast? How'd she disappear like that?"

Just as I was about to speak, the back door blew open and a torrent of wind and leaves and pine straw gushed into the kitchen. Witch Boy hopped up onto the devonette and watched in relative safety as my cousin and I rushed into the kitchen and slammed the back door shut.

Willie T. surveyed the mess that had blown in.

"Look at this!" he complained. "Looks like the whole woods is tryin' to get inside the house."

I reached up the door frame and turned the little rectangle of wood on a nail that served as a door lock, and felt a little bit safer with the door secured.

Willie T. peeped cautiously out the kitchen window.

"You reckon Erskine can get home okay, out in this?"

Looking out the window at the swaying trees and flying debris in our yard, I had to admit that I had no way in the world of knowing. But I was pretty sure that it would take more than a whirlwind to get the best of Erskine Batson.

"Reckon it's the rapture?" Willie T. asked, a look of apprehension on his face.

I stared out at the turmoil taking place outside, and tried as hard as I could to figure out what in the world my crazy cousin was talking about now.

"I don't think so," I ventured.

The boy pressed his worried face against the window pane and stared out at the chaotic scene engulfing us.

"I bet you it's the rapture, sure as the world," he insisted. "Bet you a dollar and a half it is."

Willie T., having lived his entire life thus far with Aunt Rachel as his mother, had a far greater knowledge of the Bible than I did.

"You mean like the end of the world?" I asked.

"Yeah, end of the world! Ever'body gets sucked up into the sky …"

I glared at him, eyeball to eyeball. "But, look. We're still here."

"Gyaah!" Willie T. yelped. "Ever'body got sucked up but us!"

He turned and stared back out the window. "Gyah," he complained. "I bet it even took Erskine Batson!"

My endurance had reached an end and I jabbed him in the ribs with my elbow.

"Well, let's sweep up this mess off the floor, just in case it didn't suck up Mama."

*

Willie T. agreed to help clean up the mess, just in case it really wasn't the rapture, so we set about sweeping up the leaves and trash scattered across the kitchen linoleum. Outside the wind continued to howl and rage across the mountain. The half-bare autumn trees and bushes around the house thrashed and strained like living things struggling to break loose and run away.

Squatted on the kitchen floor, holding the old worn out red tin dustpan for me, Willie T. hummed and sang "Don't mind the weather when the wind don't blow," as I swept the last bit of trash off of the linoleum.

"What I'd like to know is . . . that girl? Evy or Evergreen or whatever her dang name is? Erskine sure did seem to take a shine to her, didn't he?"

I stopped sweeping and pictured the beautiful dark skinned girl in my mind, and I remembered the way Erskine smiled when he was looking at her, out there at the old stage coach stop in the woods. His face looked as contented and happy as a hound dog layin' in the sun.

"Looked that way, didn't it?" I answered.

Willie T. dumped the shredded leaves and dirt into the kitchen trash can and gave the old dustpan a couple of thumps on the edge of the can.

"Seem like they was somethin' peculiar about her." He paused and shook his head. "She's sure enough the purtiest woman *I've* ever seen," he declared, and I glared at him, wondering when in the world he'd started paying any attention to pretty women.

"But what I want to know . . ." he continued. "Is she a real person, or is she a ghost, or what? One minute she's there, and the next dad-gummed minute she's gone? Floatin' around in the mist. Gives me the pure-dee heebie jeebies just thankin' about it." He paused and scratched his head with the edge of the dust pan. "And she was bare-footed as a haint. Nobody goes around bare-footed this time of year. Not any reg'lar person, anyway."

I thought about what he was saying, and suddenly I remembered something alarming that Mawmaw Laurie had said a while back when she was fussing about me and Willie T. spending too much time out on Moor's Gap Road.

"There's witches out there; they live out there in the woods around Moor's Gap Road," she had said. "Always have been, a whole bunch of 'em, far back as anybody can remember. You younguns better stay away from out there, or you'll wind up gettin' yourselves in a stew-pot of trouble."

I quickly decided I ought to pass this information on to Willie T.

"You reckon that girl could be a real live witch? Mawmaw says there's sure enough witches living out there, on Moor's Gap Road, just like Aunt Rachel said," I told him. "She said witches —"

A loud crash against the side of the house interrupted me, like something big and heavy had slammed against the wall with a loud *kaboom*. The two of us nearly jumped out of our skin. Witch Boy came running from the living room, yelping and skittering his toenails on the slick linoleum. He darted to the kitchen window and frantically scratched at the window sill, almost pulling the red and white checked curtains onto the floor. I grabbed him before he could destroy Mama's kitchen curtains entirely.

"Witch Boy, stay down!" I yelled at him. But he squirmed and wiggled and kept barking at something outside the window.

That's when we heard the welcome sound of Daddy's pickup truck pulling into the yard. The truck doors slammed and Mama and Daddy came tearing through the front door, accompanied by a blast of cold wind.

"Y'all okay?" Daddy called as he charged through the door with a sort of wild look on his face. He grabbed his hat off his head and slapped it against his pants leg. "Your mama and Rachel thought for sure y'all would be out in this mess!"

"We made it home okay," I answered as he wrapped me in a bone-crunching hug. He smelled like laundry starch and Camel cigarettes, and I don't think anybody in the world hugs as fiercely as my daddy.

"Erskine Batson's out there in it somewheres though," Willie T. added. "And there's witches livin' on Moor's Gap Road, sure as shootin'."

Mama and Daddy both stared at Willie T. and blinked their eyes, but neither one of them chose to respond to his announcement.

"I've never seen such a wind storm!" Mama exclaimed. She headed for the kitchen, adding under her breath, "I thought it would blow us away! Rachel was afraid it was the rapture!"

"See! I knowed it!" Willie T. gasped. "I told you so!"

Daddy laughed and shook his head. "It ain't the rapture," he assured us. "It's just a windstorm." He walked into the kitchen and peered out the window. "I *think* it's just a windstorm."

Witch Boy wagged his tail and stood up on his hind legs beside Daddy to stare out the window.

"And a big ol' limb or somethin' hit the side of the house just a minute ago," Willie T. added. "Scared the pure-dee Dickens out of us, didn't it Lily C.?"

Daddy pulled the curtain back and shifted around, looking this way and that. "I don't see anything," he told us, still peering out the window. He closed the curtains, shutting out the wild scene outside.

"I'm gonna make some popcorn," Mama announced. "Calm our nerves."

It always seemed like my mama's solution to every situation in life was popcorn.

Fourteen

A Black Coat and a High Wind

Willie T. and I relaxed a little, feeling somewhat reassured by the presence of adults in the house as the wind continued its wild howl outside. We decided to play a game of Chinese checkers, and ended up on the living room floor, whispering to each other about the possible existence of witches on the mountain, and pretending that the colored marbles were little round people from outer space.

"We need a space ship," Willie T. announced, and Daddy found us an old empty snuff can for a rocket ship and a little wooden ice cream spoon for a propeller. I don't truly believe that rocket ships are supposed to have propellers, but we made one anyway, not to hurt Daddy's feelings. We stuck the flat little wooden spoon on the lid of the snuff can with a little bitty brass nail and took turns twirling it around. I figured playing with a spaceship full of marbles and spinning our wooden propeller would be our only distraction from the awful windstorm for the rest of the afternoon. But I was wrong.

It had just started getting dark outside and Willie T. and I were still having a good time with the round marble-people from outer space, which Willie T. had named the Marbilians, when a loud knock on the front door jarred us all into the here and now. Daddy threw his newspaper down on the floor and Mama peered around the kitchen door, holding a big bowl of popcorn aloft like she might fling it at whoever it was pounding on the door. It turned out to be the Chief of Police, Clyde Tucker, tall, pot-bellied, and perpetually on the alert, in his chief-of-police uniform and cap, along with Brother Goforth, the young soft-spoken preacher from the Moonlight Ridge Baptist Church. Clyde Tucker wasted no time getting to the point.

He bobbed his head up and down a few times, looking pretty much like a long-necked turkey. "Afternoon, Sam," bobbing his head at my daddy. "Evenin', Miz Nash," bobbing at my mama. "We're goin' around to let folks know, we got us a missin' person's alert out here somewheres. Just spreadin' the word so's you can keep an eye out."

"They!" Daddy exclaimed. "A missin' person? We've had some kind of a whirlwind out on the mountain today. Who's missin'?" He craned his neck up to see outside over the police chief's shoulder. "Still whirlin', looks like."

Brother Goforth stepped forward, holding a heavy black winter coat in his hands.

"We're afraid it's Principal Vales," he said, his voice almost a whisper and a mournful hang-dog look on his face. "I just happened to be in the police station a little while ago, to report some trees and power lines down, here and there. And Miz Eudora Vales called in and said her husband was missin' —"

Me and Willie T. stopped what we were doing and stared.

"'Fessor Vales?" Daddy asked. "Well, I'll say! How long's he been missin'?"

"That's what we don't know, percisely," Clyde Tucker reported. He raised his bushy eyebrows and made a sucking noise on his front teeth. "Miz Vales has been gone from home a few days, she said. Been visitin' with some of her relations down in Eufaula, she said. And, she said, when she got home, 'Fessor Vales wadn't at the house. Said she didn't worry none till the storm hit, and when he didn't show up, she got worried and called us at the station. Said he knowed she'd be gettin' home today, and she 'spected him to be there."

Surrounded by the scattered Marbilians, Willie T. and I sat as still as church mice, as we were in the habit of doing any time big people were engaged in conversation and we didn't want to miss a single word. I saw Daddy's face twitch a little, and it looked to me like he might be trying to hold back a chuckle as he looked back and forth from the police chief to the preacher, like he was waitin' for the rest of the story.

"So what you're sayin' is that you've decided 'Fessor Vales is a missin' person because he wasn't at the house when his wife got home from visitin' her family down in Eufaula?"

Brother Goforth opened his mouth to speak, but Clyde Tucker cut him off.

"Well now, Sam, to tell you the honest truth, I wadn't too concerned about it my own self, like you say. I figgered the man's smart enough to take keer of his own self, wherever he is. But then Brother Goforth, here, wanted me to come with him to see about some power lines and trees down on this side of the mountain. An' he brung this coat with him — "

Brother Goforth hoisted up the heavy black coat for all to see.

"Found it up on the hillside, way up past Uncle Jasper's house, snagged under a great big oak tree that's down in the road. It looked to me like Principal Vales' coat. So I pulled it loose from under the tree and brought it with me to the police station . . . thought I'd turn it in."

Mama stood in the doorway between the kitchen and the living room, watching and listening. Me and Willie T. left our marble men and space ship on the floor, and we joined the men standing halfway in and halfway out the open front door. The wind outside was still flinging leaves and stray limbs all around the yard, and the screen door slammed noisily back and forth making an awful racket against the

110

front of the house. The sky was a scary sight, full of dark gray whirling clouds.

Willie T. gently ran his hand over the black coat that Brother Goforth was holding, then gave me a quizzical look. I put my hand on the coat, felt around one of the button holes, and noticed a button was missing. Without really thinking about it, I slipped my hand into a pocket and my fingers touched something that felt like a piece of paper wadded up in there. I pulled out a Hershey Bar wrapper.

Police Chief Tucker cut his eyes over at me like he was about to accuse me of tampering with evidence, and Willie T., eyebrows raised, looked at the Hershey Bar wrapper and made a loud gasping sound. Mama had slipped up behind us, still munching on a mouthful of popcorn, and she put her hand on my shoulder. Everybody looked at me, holding the wrinkled brown candy wrapper, and all of a sudden I knew for sure that it wasn't Principal Vales' coat.

"This ain't Mr. Vales's coat," Willie T. announced, shaking his head. "It ain't."

"Oh, Daddy," I managed to blurt out, holding the Hershey Bar wrapper in both my hands and inspecting it like it might have some secret message written on it. "This is Erskine's coat!"

"Erksine?" Daddy exclaimed.

"But . . . look." Brother Goforth turned the coat collar wrong-side out and revealed a name tag stitched on the lining. "EAV," he read. "Edwin Arlington Vales."

Willie T. spoke up. "It's Erskine's coat, all right. Sure as the world. Mr. Vales loaned it to him. One day at school. Tole him to keep it, didn't he, Lily C.?"

I nodded, but my cousin rushed on before I could say anything. "He was here just a little while ago, wearin' that exact same coat with the missin' button. He lost that button off the front of his coat when we all fell into . . . when he was down in . . . Well, when he was off up in the woods."

Everybody stared at Willie T.

"Up around Moor's Gap . . . the old stagecoach stop."

Police Chief Tucker made a loud whooping noise that sounded like he'd been bit by a snake or something.

"Moor's Gap? Well, I'll be a son-of-a-bitch!" he hollered. He grabbed the coat away from the preacher and shook it roughly, like he was trying to strangle somebody. "I done told that gall-durn little know-it-all bastard to stay away from up there —"

"Uhhh . . ." Daddy made a warning noise, and cut his eyes over at me and Willie T. "Don't—"

"Told him!" Clyde Tucker shouted. " 'You wanta be in trouble with the law,' I said. 'Just keep on hangin' around up there!' Up there at that . . . that . . . place!"

The police chief lolled his big old head this way and that, glared around like he suddenly couldn't focus his eyes, and let fly with a string of cuss words, many of which I'd never even heard before in my life, but I knew it was cussin'.

Brother Goforth jumped back like he'd been slapped in the face, and Daddy lowered his head and leaned forward toward the irate Clyde Tucker. That's when Witch Boy took his cue to get involved in the situation, and he leaped from the devonette like a giant flying squirrel, sailing through the air and landing square in the middle of the police chief's fat belly. The ruckus that ensued would be hard to describe, but in the middle of the melee of thrashing arms, legs, feet, fists, and dog slobber, I glanced out the open front door into the gloom and saw two men rushing across the front yard toward the house.

"Uh, y'all," I stammered, struggling to get a good grip on the rampaging brown dog. I wrestled Witch Boy down to the floor in the middle of the four pairs of scuffling feet belonging to the police chief, the preacher, my daddy, and my spluttering cousin. Mama had fled back into the kitchen and reappeared, holding the broom over her shoulder like it was a baseball bat.

"Somebody's here," I managed to sputter while holding onto the barking, snapping maniac of a dog. A second later the two men, clinging onto each other, heads down and running at top speed, clattered onto the front porch. It was Studebaker Freeman and my daddy's favorite cousin, Henry Hope Nash, a peculiar fellow if there ever was one.

The two of them were shouting the same word over and over as they crashed into the bunch of us wrestling with one another at the front door.

"Taw-nader! Taw-nader!" Studebaker yelled, jabbing at the turbulent air with his long 'magic wand' of a stick that he carried with him.

"Tor...nader! Tor...nader!" Henry Hope affirmed, clasping the wild-eyed Studebaker closer to his chest in a death grip.

We all stopped dead still in whatever awkward position we chanced to be in at the moment. Rain began pouring down in torrents, and the banging screen door sounded like shotgun blasts as it warped back and forth in the wind. Witch Boy saw his golden opportunity and made one last desperate lunge, ripped Erskine's coat out of Clyde Tucker's hands and high tailed it into the kitchen, growling and dragging the long black coat as he went.

"We all need to . . . take cover . . . somewheres!" Henry Hope yelled. He turned loose of Studebaker and grabbed ahold of the flailing screen door and tried to wrestle it shut, but it was immediately torn from his hands and went sailing through the air, landing in the front yard where it rolled end over end like a tumbling tumble weed through the wind and the rain.

The preacher and the police chief grabbed Henry Hope and Studebaker and hauled them into the living room, then Daddy managed to shove the front door closed and secured it best he could, turning the rectangle of wood on a nail that served as a door lock. Wind whistled in around the door jamb, making an ear-splitting racket that sounded for the world like a police siren. Mama threw her broom down with a clatter, then grabbed me and Willie T. by the back of our shirts and dragged us toward the kitchen.

"Under the table!" she yelled. "Under the table!" And all the men rushed in behind me and Willie T. and Mama like a human avalanche, forcing us through the door into the little kitchen.

Mama flung Willie T. and me underneath the heavy oak table like we were nothing more than Raggedy Ann and Raggedy Andy dolls, where we discovered Witch Boy curled protectively on top of Erskine's coat. He wiggled his lips up and down and growled, baring his teeth. Then the six adults dove under, shoving me and my squirming cousin and the growling dog flat as flitters against the kitchen wall. Witch Boy yelped a pitiful note, then grabbed a slobbery mouthful of my hair and began shaking and pulling like he intended to snatch me bald-headed.

There was a horrible deafening noise outside that sounded like a great big freight train headed straight for our house.

"Lord! Look down upon us, Lord, in our pitiful condition, Lord . . ." Brother Goforth called out, his face turned up toward the underside of our kitchen table like it was the Glory Land. I couldn't help but take note of several gray wads of petrified Juicy Fruit Chewing Gum stuck along the sides of the tabletop.

"Just save us tonight . . . Lord," Henry Hope added. "Just . . . save us tonight!"

I elbowed Witch Boy in the ribs best I could, and just as I got him to turn loose of my hair, Willie T. clinched his arm around my neck so tight I couldn't hardly breathe, and I was getting nowhere trying to prize him aloose. I quickly gave up and decided if we were all about to die in a tornado anyway, it wouldn't hurt me any worse to be choked to death. I figured the last sight I'd see in this world was Willie T.'s terrified eyeballs, big around as baseballs, and it suddenly made me think of Bu, our old hoot-owl out in the woods.

"Reckon how old Bu is fairing through all this?" I croaked, trying once again to get free of Willie T.'s choke hold.

Willie T. relaxed his grip, and wiped his sweaty face with the sleeve of his flannel shirt. "Pulverized, most likely," he replied, shaking his head.

The wind kept howling and Brother Goforth kept praying. Then, just when I was pretty sure that our end was at hand, like some kind of unbelievable miracle, the wind died down and everything got completely quiet and still. For a few seconds we all held our breath and listened to the quiet, not hardly able to believe our ears.

"Is that it?" Mama asked.

"I believe it is," Daddy responded as he unfolded his self out from under the table. Police Chief Clyde Tucker, Brother Goforth, Studebaker Freeman, Henry Hope Nash, and my mama crawled out one at a time on all fours, then Daddy reached under the table and pulled me and Willie T. out.

"Y'all ain't squinched to death, are you?" he asked, running his hand through my dog-slobbery hair in a more-or-less absent minded gesture.

"Near about," Willie T. answered, rubbing both his hands across his bristly flat-top hair cut.

Witch Boy let out a couple of exasperated barks, planted his front feet firmly on the black coat, and refused to come out from under the table.

"Well, let's see what she looks like," Daddy sighed, and headed for the back door.

Fifteen

What She Looked Like

Doom and disaster, that's what she looked like. Outside, everything was dark and wet and if there was a limb left on a tree, you couldn't prove it by me. Little limbs and big ones were scattered all over the place and the whole yard was covered with jillions of little white balls of icy hail.

"They — " Daddy sighed in a long, drawn out breath.

After all the noise and commotion of the storm, now everything was eerily silent and still. We all stood peering out the back door like a bunch of beady-eyed chickens staring at the chop block. Willie T., standing right behind me, laid his cheek against my shoulder and whispered, "The rapture … I knowed it."

That was my last straw.

I elbowed him in the ribs about as hard as I could, but he just broke out laughing and snickering, pointing at my head.

"Aunt Sara! Lookee there at Lily Claire's head!" he sputtered.

Mama cut her eyes in my direction in a more-or-less slack jawed gaze, like she was in such a state she couldn't decide whether or not I was worth lookin' at, what with all the destruction of the world outside.

"Well, Lily Claire!" was all she chose to say, then she followed all the men out onto the back porch to get a better view of the aftermath.

Willie T. and I followed them out, and as we surveyed the jumble of storm leavings in the yard, I tried to run my fingers through my hair to straighten it out a little; but the dog slobber had glommed up into sticky clumps and tangles, stiff as a board. I truly believe dog slobber could prove to be a fairly good substitute for Helene Curtis spray net.

A loud, whooping noise in the distance caught our attention, and way up the hill, Papa Jasper and Mawmaw Laurie appeared on their front porch. I could barely see them through the gloom, but I could see Mawmaw's white handkerchief as she fluttered it at us in a sort of casual, friendly way, while Papa Jasper waved both his arms over his head and let out a couple of "Whoo-ooo, whoo-ooo!" calls to signal us.

"We're all right up here. Y'all all right down there?" Mawmaw hollered pleasantly after Papa had stopped hooting. I reckon it takes more than a rapture storm to ruffle her nerves.

Daddy waved back and yelled, "We're all fine! Fine!"

"Chicken coop's blowed away," Mawmaw yelled. "Y'all want to come help catch the hens in the morning?" She flapped her handkerchief in the air like she was swatting at something. "They'll be all right till morning," she added.

Clyde Tucker cleared his throat and spit over the side of the porch. "Well, now. I believe I'd best be gettin' back to Eden, see what's what," he announced. He pulled his hat off and wiped his oily head with his forearm, then replaced the hat. "But I'll tell you what! Mark my word, t'morrer, first thang in the mornin', I'm goin' up there and take care of that bidness at Moor's Gap. If he ain't dead up there under a fell down tree or somethin', I'll have me a talk with Mr. Big Ike, Erskine Batson! Ain't nobody got no bidness hangin' around up there . . . messin' around where they don't belong.

117

"Come on, Preacher," he growled. "You goin' back with me?"

Brother Goforth allowed that he reckoned he would.

"Good Lord bless and keep you all. Glad everybody's safe and sound here," he said. We watched as the preacher and the police chief picked their way across the dark littered yard, pointing and exclaiming as they went. Then Police Chief Clyde Tucker turned on his flashing lights and his police siren and bounced the roaring vehicle through mud and over tree limbs as they disappeared into the night.

"Lord have mercy," Mama sighed as we all trailed back into the kitchen. Daddy closed the back door and shook his head. "I'll swear . . ." was all he said.

"Save us and . . . bind us," Henry Hope added, bobbing his head up and down in agreement.

"Wrong time a' year for a taw-nader," Studebaker remarked in a low, ominous voice. "Somethin's sure 'nough wrong out here on this mountain, I tell you that's the truth!"

I felt pretty sure that he was right about that.

"And that smart-alecky white-cracker school teacher, in trouble *again*? Up there somewhere in the woods, I suspect," he grumbled. "Pokin' round where he don't belong to poke."

Daddy shook his head again and said "Um, umm, um!"

By that time we were all so wore to a frazzle, we could all just about faint and fall back in it. Witch Boy crept out from under the kitchen table and proceeded to scratch on the back door, whining like he needed to go out. But then when he saw how things were outside, he turned around and headed into the living room, toenails clicking on the linoleum as he went, and flopped his self down under mama's coffee table.

The perilous night ended when Henry Hope and Studebaker decided to head on back to Henry Hope's house in town and make sure everything was still in one piece, and Uncle Buddy Nock, waving a flashlight around in the dark, appeared on our front porch to reclaim Willie T. and carry him home where, Uncle Buddy reported, Aunt Rachel was having a nervous breakdown over the storm. Their electricity had gone off, he said, and tonight was the night that a television show called "The Other Side of the Moon" was supposed to be on the *Science Fiction The-ater*.

Willie T. showed no signs of joy about going home, with no *Science Fiction The-ater* to look forward to, and all the excitement of the storm and the falling trees and the lost school teacher and the escaped chickens to deal with. But he reluctantly gave in and went on with Uncle Buddy anyway.

After everybody had left and all the tornado excitement died down a little, Mama laid down the law and made me wash my dog-slobbery hair in the kitchen sink. Then she turned on the Hot Point oven and sat with me until my hair was dry and I was as drowsy as a chicken on the roost. Mama gave me a hug and said, "Now, that looks better," and I drug myself off to bed.

"Cold as hell, clear as a bell, and everything smells like popcorn," I muttered to myself as I crawled into bed. Daddy poked his head in my room and asked, "What's that?" with a tired chuckle, then he helped me get hunkered down under two warm quilts, my red calico Drunkard's Path and a blue and white Storm at Sea. He pulled the quilts up under my chin, patted my head like he always did, the way you'd pat a dog or a puppy, and warned me to keep my elbows covered up because people catch cold through their elbows.

The rest of the night was cold, pitch black, and deadly quiet.

For a little while I couldn't stop worrying about Erskine Batson, off in the woods somewhere, maybe crushed under a fallen tree like Clyde Tucker had said, and I wondered why the police chief was so mad about Erskine spending time messing around like he did at Moor's Gap. But then I drifted off to sleep with the Storm at Sea quilt pulled over my head, and I dreamed about a big black crow, flying alone through a terrible storm over the other side of the moon, carrying a big piece of popcorn in his beak.

Sixteen

Climbing Cat Bluff

The next morning was windy and cold with a clear blue sky. Daddy was gone to work in Roebuck, a little place outside Birmingham, where they were building a circular bank building. He told us it was the first time he'd ever seen anybody build a round bank building, and he talked about it like it was one of the seven wonders of the world. Mama woke me up early to tell me she was going up the hill to help round up Mawmaw's blowed-away chickens.

I pulled the covers up around my neck and burrowed my head into my pillow, listening to the wind and watching the bare trees sway and shake outside my bedroom window. I was glad that it was Thanksgiving Holidays, and we wouldn't have to go to school for the entire week. Snuggled down in my warm bed, with the quilts soft and cozy around me, I thought about how strange the quiet, empty classrooms must look, with all the rows of desks empty and no students and no teachers —

With a shock I remembered that Erskine was lost somewhere out on the mountain.

Leaping out of bed, I stepped right on Witch Boy who was sleeping on the little rag rug beside my bed where I didn't expect him to be. He yelped and skittered around, snapping at my ankle, then he stretched and yawned and shook himself all up and down.

Shivering in the chilly bedroom, I got into my clothes as fast as I could: long blue poplin pants lined on the inside with red plaid flannel, a white cowboy shirt with pearl snaps up the front, and brown leather Buster Brown oxfords. My heart felt like it would pound out of my chest as I imagined our teacher somewhere out in the damp windy woods, in one kind of a predicament or another. A sudden vision of our near-disaster on Halloween just a few weeks before brought panicky tears to my eyes. Surely, surely, I thought, Erskine couldn't have found another dad-blamed hole to fall into!

In the kitchen I found some biscuits and a plate of crispy bacon still warm on the stove. I touched the side of the coffee pot and it felt warm enough, so I poured myself half a cup of coffee, adding enough canned Pet Milk and sugar to make a delicious caramel flavored concoction. When I opened the back door just a crack to let Witch Boy out, cold sharp wind whipped into the kitchen, causing me to shiver. Witch Boy bounded across the yard, dancing and barking at nothing in particular in the clear cold air.

As I expected, Willie T. showed up while I was eating breakfast, and he helped himself to a biscuit with a long piece of bacon dangling out of it, and a cup full to the brim with coffee, Pet Milk, and sugar.

"We gonna help Aunt Laurie and Uncle Jasper catch the chickie-chickies?" he asked, biscuit crumbs a'flying.

But chickens were the last thing on my mind.

"We need to go see if we can find Erskine," I told him. "He must be in some kind of trouble, or lost, or something awful!"

Willie T. stuffed the rest of his biscuit and bacon into his mouth, then craned his neck out like a chicken trying to swallow the dry mouthful.

121

"Well, let's get goin' then!" he spluttered. "I sure as the Dickens hope he ain't fell in no 'nuther dang hole again!"

I had to admit that I had been thinking that exact same thought myself, all morning long.

When we grabbed our jackets and toboggan caps, we discovered Erskine's long black coat hanging on a nail by the back door. Willie T. folded and rolled the heavy coat into a tidy bundle, tied it together with the two long coat sleeves, and hung it over his shoulders like a backpack. We hurried out the door, headed for Moor's Gap with no idea of what we might find. Witch Boy loped along with us, in a gay adventurous mood, smelling the ground and running ahead of us on the dirt road, stopping every now and then to sniff the air and bark.

The cold autumn wind seemed to be blowing from every direction, first in our faces, then pushing at our backs as we clambered up the mountain road, jumping over fallen limbs and piles of wet leaves and pine cones scattered everywhere. We tried to avoid the worst of the sticky mud and slushy potholes, but we weren't one hundred percent successful in that hopeless attempt.

"Look out for the ruts!" Willie T. shouted after tearing through a particularly sloppy bog of red mud. "My shoes is already rurnt!" he observed.

We passed by a big cedar tree, still bushy and green even after the fierce storm, with our splintered and twisted screen door stuck way up in the top of the tree and swayin' in the wind. Dozens of squirrels were scampering in every direction, chattering and fussing.

And crows? I've never seen the like! A whole flock of the huge black creatures kept up an eardrum splitting racket as they flew restlessly from tree to tree, cawing and hollering back and forth at one another.

"Dang birds!" Willie T. complained, pointing up towards one exceptionally large and noisy individual. "I believe to my soul, that's the one that was so friendly with that Evy girl . . .

and the one that broke into your bedroom. Don't he look familiar?"

At that moment, the very bird that Willie T. was pointing at came swooping down toward us, cawing and yelling louder than ever.

"What? What? What?" the bird croaked.

Witch Boy joined in, barking as loud as he possibly could, as the huge black crow dove straight at us then veered off and lit on a straggly looking limb over our heads.

"Caw, caw!" he screamed, fixing us with his glassy black eyes.

"Midnight?" I called, curious to see if he recognized his name. "Midnight, is that you?"

Before you could say Jack Robinson, the giant black bird dove toward us again, then flew a few yards away and lit on top of a big rock boulder beside the trail, where he raised his wings and shook himself all over like a big black dog. Witch Boy let loose with a conniption fit of loud barking, then ran toward the boulder and started trying to climb up the steep side of the big rock. As my cousin and I watched, the crow swooped down and snatched a claw full of the dog's brown fur, then flew further down the trail. Witch Boy yelped, and ran after the crow.

"I think he's trying to make us foller him," Willie T. said. Then he yelled up at the crow, "We was goin' that way anyways, stupid bird!"

When we reached the cutoff that led up to the tumble-down stage coach inn, just as I had expected he would do, the crow flew in that direction and perched on the low rock wall, looking pretty pleased with himself for waiting for us. He pecked around on the rocks with his gigantic beak, then began strolling up and down, from one corner of the wall to the other, while Willie T. and I surveyed the scattered mess the storm had made of our clubhouse. Everything was covered with broken tree limbs and wet leaves, pine cones and wads of pine straw. A cold wind blew, making the tall pine trees and cedars bow and sway around us. Bunches of low clouds flew across the cold blue sky, blocking the sun and casting their gray shadows over the wet and dreary landscape.

Midnight launched up into the air and tried to land on top of Willie T.'s head, causing my cousin to flail his arms like a crazy man, cussing and yelling. You wouldn't believe just how big a crow really is till you see one up close trying to land on your cousin's head.

Of course, Witch Boy thought it was the best thing he'd ever seen, and he fell into a joyful fit of barking and dancing. Then, without a warning, the crow took off up the hill toward the high ridge, way up at the top of the mountain.

Willie T. and I trudged through the wet bushes, in the very place where we had first seen the strange girl appear out of the fog.

"Why are we goin' this a'way?" Willie T. whined. "Ain't nothin' but wet weeds and beggar lice. Ain't even hardly no trail . . . hardly," he added as we both looked down at our feet and discovered that there actually was a faint old trail, leading up toward the bluff above us.

"Gyah!" Willie T. exclaimed, all of a sudden stopping in his tracks without a warning. "Look up yonder, Lily C. See them big rocks up there? You know what that is, don't you?"

I gazed up at the big old black rocks way up at the top of the ridge above us.

"Cat Bluff," I whispered.

"Cat Bluff!" my cousin blurted out in the most exasperated voice you could imagine. He turned his head this way and that, gazing up at the swaying trees around us.

"Where's that dang bird?" he yelped. "I ain't goin' to no Cat Bluff to get us both eat up by no black panther! No-siree-bob-tail!"

I had to admit it seemed like a bad way to go. But I still felt like we needed to see if the crow really was leading us somewhere, and I sure didn't want us to give up on trying to find our teacher, wherever he was.

"If we make a big noise, it'll scare all the panthers and mountain lions and bobcats away from us," I suggested. "And you remember how Henry Hope and I yelled out your name, over and over, when you fell down in the old church well and we were tryin' to find you?"

Willie T. stomped the ground and pulled up a handful of dead weeds then threw them down like he was purely disgusted. "Yeah, I heard y'all callin' me, and I was purty glad to know that y'all was lookin' for me."

"Well, if we call out Erskine's name as we climb up to the bluff, if he's around here anywhere maybe he'll hear us and be glad we're lookin' for him; and we'll scare off the painters at the same time," I said, using the old-fashioned way of sayin' painter instead of panther, just to give my cousin a little boost.

I guess it boosted him, because he sighed and stomped the ground again, then said, "All right then. Maybe that'll work. But if we get eat up by painters and our blood and guts is strowed all up and down the mountainside, don't blame me!"

The rest of the way up the mountain was rough going, following the weedy, scraggly old trail up toward the great big scary looking rocks above us. And we both realized right off that we were being watched and followed by something that stayed just out of sight in the thick bushes beside the trail.

"Erskine Batson!" I called out into the blustery woods, and "Teacher! Where the tarnation are you?" Willie T. hollered. And the big black crow flapped from tree branch to tree branch, making the awfullest racket in the world. And Witch Boy was baying like a hound dog chasing a raccoon! I hoped that maybe every wild cat in Alabama would be scared half to death when they heard us scrambling up the mountain, making such a raucous commotion. But Willie T. stopped and cast his eyes over toward a thick clump of bushes and said he thought it would probably just call all the snarling hungry critters to us. I hoped he was wrong. Then, wouldn't you know it, as we fought our way up the steep path, thinking every minute might be our last, Willie T. decided to tell one of Mawmaw's favorite scary stories, the scariest story he could think of to tell.

Seventeen

The Painter's Toe

Way back yonder a long time ago, there was an old man and an old woman livin' not too far from here, and they had a big garden full of turnip greens growin' behind their house. And every day the old woman would go out with a big sharp butcher knife and cut a mess of turnip greens to cook for their supper.

Then one day she went out late in the evenin', just when it was gettin' dark, to cut her a bunch of turnip greens, and she didn't know it, but there was a big black painter sleepin' on the cool ground underneath a great big old bunch of turnip greens. He'd crawled up under there and gone to sleep where there was a little bit of shade. He went sound asleep with one big foot sticking out from under the bunch of turnip greens.

So when the old woman came along, she saw the painter's big old toe sticking out from under the green leaves, and in the dark she thought it was a big turnip! "My, that's a big tasty lookin' turnip!" she said. And she cut off the painter's toe with her butcher knife and dropped it in the bucket with the turnip greens. That evenin' when she went to cook supper, she found the painter's toe in the bucket, and she said, "I'll use this to season the pot!"

And so she cooked the painter's toe in the pot full of greens.

That evenin' at supper time, the old man came home and went to eatin' his greens and cornbread, and he smacked his old lips and said, "This is the tastiest mess of turnip greens I ever ate in my life!"

So the old man and the old woman finished their supper, and the old woman washed up the dishes and the pots and pans, and they went to bed, thinkin' they'd have a good night's sleep after that delicious supper.

But way in the middle of the night, it was dark and cold and the old man and old woman were all covered up in their bed, they heard a deep scary voice that said,

"I wannnnt myyy big toe!"

Well, it was the awfullest sound they'd ever heard, and the old woman said "Get up old man, and see what that noise is!"

So the old man got up and looked around. He looked under the bed, and he looked under the chest of drawers, and he looked behind the curtains, and he couldn't find anything. So he got back into bed and went back to sleep.

About that time, they heard it again.

"I wannnt myyy big toe!"

The old man said "Get up old woman, and see what that noise is!"

So the old woman got up, and she looked under the stove and she looked under the kitchen table, and she didn't find anything. So she hurried back to bed and jumped under the covers and went back to sleep.

Pretty soon, it woke them up again, with the awfullest moanin' sound either one of them had ever heard.

"I wannnt myyy big toe!"

By this time they were both scared and the old woman wasn't about to get up again, so she said, "Get up old man, and see what that noise is."

So the old man got up and crept into the dark kitchen and looked all around, and didn't see anything. Then he opened up the pantry, and there it sat! Up on the top shelf of the pantry sat the biggest blackest painter he'd ever seen in his life. And it looked right at him and blew its awful breath right in his face and moaned,

"I wannnt myyy big toe!"

Well, the old man was so scared he was just a'shakin' and he looked at the big ol' painter sittin' up there in the dark, and he asked,

"What's them big eyes for?"

And the painter growled, "To see you with."

Then the old man took another look at the painter, and asked,

"What's that big nose for?"

The painter said, "To smell your blood."

"What's them big claws for?" the old man asked.

The painter set his eyes right on the old man and said, "To dig yo' grave."

Then the old man asked, "What's that long beard for?

The painter said, "To sweep yo' grave."

Then the old man said, "Well, what's them long tusks for?"

The painter JUMPED down and grabbed him and growled,

"TO EAT YOU UP!"

Of course, when Willie T. jumped and grabbed me and yelled "TO EAT YOU UP," it scared the daylights out of me like it always did, making me jump ten feet in the air and scream bloody murder. No matter how many times you hear the story about the painter's toe, you can't help but scream when the painter growls "To eat you up!"

We reached the top of the bluff with my nerves in a dither and Willie T. laughing and snickering like a maniac. We climbed out onto a big overhanging rock, jagged and pretty much sticking out into thin air, that looked amazingly like a huge crouching panther. From that vantage point, we could see all the way back down the mountain. Over the tops of the swaying trees we were able to see the tumbled down walls of the old stage coach inn, Moor's Gap Road as it ran from one side of the mountain to the other, and three scrambling men, looking tiny and peculiar in the lower distance, headed in our direction!

"Now who the dang Sam Hill is that?" Willie T. griped, leaning way out over the edge of the cat-shaped boulder and wrinkling up his eyebrows. "That ain't Erskine down there, is it?"

I held a good grip on my cousin's arm and stared down over the side of Cat Bluff at the men down below us as they thrashed their way in and out of the bushes.

I recognized one of them.

"Oh, no!" I gasped, gripping Willie T.'s arm a little tighter. "It's Clyde Tucker!"

Willie T. snorted like a stuck hog and threw his arms up in the air so fast he almost knocked me over the edge of the cliff. My feet slipped on the loose gravel and wet leaves, and I floundered so close to the drop-off that I like to had a heart attack, and for a split second I thought for sure that I'd met my Waterloo! Just in the nick of time, Willie T. grabbed the back of my coat and yanked me backwards away from the brink of death, and I wobbled around like a chicken with its head cut off until I managed to regain my balance. It scared me so bad that tears sprung up in my eyes, and I gulped and swallowed, trying to stop myself from sobbing. I doubled up my fist and took a swing at Willie T., catching him right on the side of his head, but his old toboggan cap was so thick, and his skull to boot, it didn't hardly faze him at all.

"Lord a'mighty, Lily C.!" he complained, straightening his cap. "Don't get so close't to the edge!"

All the commotion had caused Witch Boy to jump around, growling and snapping.

"Shh, shh, get quiet, dog," Willie T. whispered, patting and quieting the dog. "What the dang Dickens do you reckon that stupid Sheriff Clyde Tucker is doin' up here?" Witch Boy lay down flat on his belly like a lizard and stuck his head over the edge of the rock to see what he could see. While I struggled to catch my breath and waited for my legs to quit shaking, we watched the three men as they milled around in the bushes, stomping and thrashing their arms like they were searching for something on the ground. Then they all sat down on the old rock wall and commenced to light up cigarettes and started talking among themselves, gesturing and pointing first one way then another. The sound of their voices carried up to us, but it was too far away to tell what they were saying. None of them looked up in our direction.

I narrowed my eyes, wiped away a few damp tears, and focused my gaze on one of the men sitting beside Police Chief Tucker. "Look," I whispered. "That's Olie Hutchins down there."

Willie T. and I squatted down beside Witch Boy, and we stared down at the three men sitting in a row like three lost buzzards on a limb.

"Olie Hutchins? It's that Ku Klux man, ain't it? Now what do you reckon he's up here for?" Willie T. spat on the ground.

"Stickin' his big nose into everybody else's business, like he always does," I said. "And look. That's Brother Goforth with them. I bet they're searchin' for Erskine."

Willie T. nudged me with his elbow. "I don't thank they know we're up here, you know it, Lily C.?" he whispered. "Let's go on up the trail."

We inched back away from the edge of the bluff and stood, brushing dead leaves and dirt from our coats and pants legs. I looked around me in all directions.

"What trail?" I asked, pulling my jacket tighter around me. A blast of icy wind whipped through the woods and tugged at my clothes. Willie T. and I both adjusted our toboggan caps and Witch Boy snorted in the cold wind and shook himself all up and down.

"Lordy, it's cold out here!" my cousin announced. "Cold as a witch's teat!" His cheeks were as red as Mawmaw's baking apples. "Did we lose the trail?" he complained, slapping at a bunch of tall dead weeds in a hopeless gesture.

The smart-alecky crow appeared, perched on a swaying black limb above our heads, and gave a startling cry.

"Where, where, where, where!" he cawed, then fluttered away, disappearing into the deep woods.

"Come on," Willie T. muttered. "This a'way."

And we followed the crow.

Eighteen

A Strange Encounter

I can't begin to explain it, but as we trudged our way through the wet scratchy bushes, dodging low hanging tree limbs and following a barely visible path covered with wet leaves, the woods got darker and darker till it looked like twilight all around us. I reared my head back to see if I could locate the sun and try to determine what time of day it was, but the trees were too tall and the clouds overhead were too thick and gray. Willie T. didn't say a word, and the only sound was our huffing and puffing as we fought our way through the brush. Then Witch Boy commenced to whine and whimper in the most nerve wracking way you could imagine, and it set my nerves to jittering worse than they already had been.

"What the . . ." Willie T. began, glancing down at the whimpering dog as we rounded a bend in the trail. But before he could finish his question, I screamed and jumped backwards and Witch Boy yelped like he'd been kicked. Willie T. grabbed ahold of me and we both gawked at the sight of a rumpled and raggedy man sitting on a big rock in the dim shadows ahead of us.

For just a second I thought for sure it was the loup-garou.

"The lord a'mercy!" Willie T. gasped. Then he leaned forward to get a better look at the nasty looking fellow, dressed in awful looking old overalls and a raggedy old holey undershirt, covered with dirt and stains.

"The lord a'mercy," he repeated, and a chill ran down my backbone because I suddenly knew what his next words were going to be.

"Possum Man? . . . Possum Man? . . . Joe John Lee! Is it you?"

The man barely moved, just stared at us with a sly looking grin on his face and a long thin twig sticking out of his lop-sided mouth.

His grin widened into a mean looking smirk from jaw hinge to jaw hinge.

"Whar you yangerns goin'?" he asked in a creepy-sounding unfriendly voice.

Witch Boy pressed up close to my legs and let out a low rumbling growl.

"We ain't goin' nowheres," Willie T. announced defensively. "Are *you* the Possum Man?"

"He he he," the man wheezed in a mocking laugh. The twig in his mouth bobbed up and down. "What you yangerns doin', out hyar in the woods, all by ye'selves? Hm? Y'all gwine up thar to them witches?"

Willie T. and I both caught our breath and quickly gazed up the trail toward the top of the mountain.

"What witches? We ain't goin' . . . We're just out walkin' around," my cousin stammered.

"We're lookin' for somebody," I managed to say. I scraped up whatever courage I could and asked, "Are you Joe John Lee? We heard you were dead . . ."

A loud gust of cold wind swept up through the trees, shaking the few remaining dead leaves off the tree limbs and blowing so hard it nearly knocked me and Willie T. off our feet. Witch Boy began pacing around my legs in an angry, protective circle.

The man squinted his dark greasy looking eyes and continued grinning at us, somehow managing to grin and look dangerous at the same time.

"Gwine up thar to them black witches," he stated with a wicked smirk, nodding his head up and down.

A look of revelation came over Willie T.'s face. "You mean that black girl? Evy?" he asked, shifting his gaze from the scary looking man to the thick dark woods ahead of us, then back again. "She's . . . well, at first . . . we thought she was a . . . a ghost . . . or somethin'."

This brought on a horrible outburst of evil sounding laughter from the man. He narrowed his eyes and shifted the twig in his mouth from side to side. "You'uns believe in ghosts, do ye?" He rocked back and forth and kept laughing in his wheezy cackle. "She's *somethin'*, all right! But she ain't no ghost!"

Suddenly Willie T. slapped both his hands against my back and pushed me up the trail, forcing me to stumble along with the dog still circling and rubbing against my legs.

"Let's go, Lily C.," he muttered under his breath. "We need to get from here."

The cackling laughter followed us as we scrambled away, walking as fast as our scared-stiff legs could carry us. Hearing a rustling in the bushes behind us, I turned and looked, hoping we weren't about to be grabbed from behind. There wasn't a soul in sight.

"Look, Willie T.," I whispered. "He's gone!"

My cousin turned and looked over his shoulder without a word, and continued to shove me forward, deeper into the dark and dreary woods.

After we had put some distance between us and the gruesome apparition, whoever he was, we stopped and drew a few shaky breaths.

"I swear, Lily C., I believe that was the Possum Man! I *know* it was. Joe John Lee as plain as day."

I shivered and pulled my coat closer around me.

"But, Willie T., it couldn't be him. I promise for certain, Daddy told us that somebody had found Possum Man out in the woods, dead . . . all by his self and all his possums were nowhere to be seen. It was about a year ago."

"Yeah, that's what my daddy said, too. I asked him about it, a while back when you and me had been talking about the Possum Man. He said some men was out huntin', and sure enough they found Possum Man, layin' on the ground out in the woods, dead and all rotted away somethin' awful . . . and whatever and all." Willie T. paused and looked back behind us again. "But I *know* that was him, Lily C. Sure enough *looked* like him. Plain as day." He shook his head, then looked at the darkening woods around us. "I wish't we had a watch or somethin'. Look how dark it's gettin'."

I sighed and gazed up at the twisted black limbs and wintery trees swaying in the cold wind. Low and behold, there sat Midnight, the crow, perched on a bare tree limb right above our heads and staring down his long beak at us.

Willie T. whooped.

"What the dang Sam Hill? Where did you come from, like a thief in the night?"

The crow bobbed up and down on the tree limb and let out a shriek that coulda woke the dead, then he flew off into the woods and everything around us became totally quiet. Witch Boy lowered his head and padded away in the direction the crow had gone.

Willie T. grabbed ahold of my coat sleeve and gave it a little shake. "Listen," he whispered.

I listened, and at first I heard absolutely nothing. Then, I thought I could hear voices, off in the woods just a little ways ahead of us. Someone singing maybe. It sounded like a bunch of voices , chanting.

We stood still, listening to the strange voices, then Willie T. raised his eyebrows up and glanced at me sideways. "I thank we ort to go on back home . . . I'm froze nearly to death, and I bet you a dollar and a half, it's them witches." He shivered so hard I heard his teeth chattering.

Just at that moment I was inclined to agree. I don't think I'd ever heard anything as hair-raising as that spooky-sounding singing, high and plaintive notes drifting through the cold windy woods. I couldn't make out the words at all, but the sound was something like a slow, sad church hymn.

"Gyah . . ." Willie T. breathed, taking a few steps backwards as if he intended to take off back down the trail the way we had come. "I'd as soon be listenin' to the wolfeener a'howlin'."

We both stood still, listening, as the peculiar singing drifted away and the woods around us grew hushed and still. Just when everything was totally quiet, suddenly a bird in the tree above us broke into a trill so loud it made us both just about jump out of our skin.

"Secret, secret, secret!" the bird chirped, loud enough to split your eardrums. "Secret, secret, secret, secret!"

"Lord a'mercy!" Willie T. exclaimed, casting his eyes all around.

"Secret, secret, secret!" the bird called again, waking me up out of whatever strange spell the eerie singing had cast over me.

"We've come this far," I sighed. "I think we ought to go on far enough to see who that is singin'."

My cousin gave me a grimacing stare and yanked his toboggan cap off his head. He spluttered and grunted like he was trying to think of something to say, clawed at his scalp, and then jammed his toboggan back on his head.

"All right, then!" he barked. "But what if it *is* witches, like . . . like that man said?"

I considered that possibility for a few seconds. "Well, let's try to sneak up on 'em, real quiet. Maybe we can stay hid in the bushes, and get a peak at whoever it is. . . without them seein' us?"

Willie T. snorted and huffed. "I thought we was s'pose to be out here lookin' for Erskine Batson . . . lost out here somewheres in the storm. I sure as shootin' don't want to get into it with no blamed witches! This ain't got nothin' to do with no lost school teacher, I don't thank!"

I wondered if he might be right, and hesitated long enough to consider whether to go ahead and take a look, or turn around and run for our lives, back down the mountainside.

"Secret, secret, secret!" the noisy little bird called again, then flew silently away from us, into the woods.

"I just got a feelin'," I whispered.

And we picked our way through the trees and dead winter bushes, in the direction of the singing voices.

Nineteen

The Wayward Sisters

Willie T. and I had gone just a few steps, pushing briars and brambles out of our way as we got closer to the place where the mysterious singing voices were coming from, when I heard something moving through the thicket close to us. It sounded like something big.

We both stopped and looked at each other.

"Was that Witch Boy?" my cousin whispered.

"I don't know," I whispered back, afraid to move another inch. "I don't think so."

The bushes rustled again as something moved closer to us, and whatever it was, it made a noise that sounded like a loud rattling purr. I knew dogs don't purr, and it sounded bigger than any cat I had ever seen or heard. I caught just a quick glimpse of a large black shape as it moved toward us then disappeared from sight under a big cedar tree.

"It's a big black panther, sure as the world," Willie T. breathed, and I was awfully afraid that he was right.

"Get away from here, you old painter!" he yelled, waving his arms up and down toward the bushes. "We ain't got your ol' big toe!"

We waited and listened, but didn't hear any more rustling noises, and nothing jumped out to get us, yet.

Willie T. let out a loud breath. "Whew! Let's go on and see who's out here in the woods makin' those sangin' noises. It's better than standin' here and waitin' to get eat up."

Just then, the voices started up singing again, and I grabbed my cousin's arm and we both hunkered down low to the ground and sneaked toward the sound of a plaintive refrain.

We are . . . we are
climbing . . . climbing
Jacob's . . .
ladder . . .
We are . . . we are
climbing . . . climbing
Jacob's . . .
ladder . . .

Following the voices, we pushed our way through a clump of cherry laurels and privet hedges, and found ourselves peering through the bushes at the edge of a clearing. There in the middle of a wide dirt yard sat a little ramshackle cabin, raised up high off the ground on precarious looking rock piers, with a set of high wooden steps leading up to the front porch. Smoke puffed peacefully from a tall rock chimney at one end of the dark little house, and a huge black crow was perched on the sharp ridge of the gray tin roof. A few confused looking chickens strolled around the yard, looking bored and pecking the ground.

Willie T. and I stayed where we were, partially hidden in the bushes at the edge of the yard, both of us eyeballing the scene before us as the singing continued at a strident pitch.

We are! . . . we are
climbing! . . . climbing

Jacob's !
ladder!
Soldiers . . .
of the . . .
cross .

It was three black women gathered out in the yard. Two of them stood side by side, dressed in long wool coats and bare-footed as haints, with their arms wrapped around one another, watching the third who stood beside a big round black pot, stirring whatever was in the pot with a long wooden pole. A near-burned-out fire, mostly coals and ashes, smoldered under the large pot.

"Gots to get these clothes out dis pot, hung up to dry, so's I can clean out de pot. I'm 'bout fin' to cook me up some chitterlins, 'fore de foul weather break loose."

"Foul weather," the other two women repeated together in soft, dreamy sounding voices. "Foul is fair, and fair is foul."

Beside me, Willie T. gasped and jabbed me with his elbow.

"Did you hear that?" he squeaked. "She said she's about to cook up some childrens in that pot!"

I glared at my cousin's startled face. His eyeballs were big around as cannon balls and his mouth hung open in alarm.

"I don't think she . . ." I started to reply, but he butted in, nodding his head up and down vigorously.

"I knowed it! Witches! Witches gonna cook us in a pot! See what we done got into? Tole you we shoulda gone back . . . I knowed it!"

Just then the woman stirring the pot called out in a loud, clear voice.

"Whoever you is, you sho' better come on out dem bushes 'fore you gets savored by a painter."

"Uh oh! They seen us," Willie T. groaned.

141

"Don't has to see you," the woman replied. "Hear'd you comin' up that mountain, all mawnin' long! Lassander! Get yo' brown self out here!"

Willie T. and I looked at each other.

Witch Boy's ears shot up straight above his knobby head and he launched out of the bushes like a race horse. He skidded past the simmering pot and landed at the feet of the two women standing together, where he fell on the ground and commenced kicking all four feet up and down in the air. Chickens scattered in all directions. The two women, with their arms still wrapped around each other, calmly stared down at the crazy dog writhing at their feet.

"There you is," the pretty young girl crooned in a voice that sounded musical, sweet, and familiar. I recognized that voice.

"Why, that's Evy!" I exclaimed, grabbing my cousin's arm and hauling him out into the clearing. Willie T. yelped.

"It's Evy," I repeated, tugging him along with me toward the three women standing in front of the little wooden cabin. We got close enough for me to see that, sure enough, it was Evy, wearing the red ruby ear bobs.

Witch Boy sat up at the women's feet and looked at us and snorted. The woman at the pot continued to stir slowly with her long wooden pole, then shook her head and laughed.

"So, it's y'all. Scalawag chilluns! Y'all de scholars, then?"

Willie T. and I both stiffened and cut our eyes around at each other.

"Scholars?" I exclaimed. "Who told you that?"

The woman stirring the pot and the two hugging women blinked their eyes and stared at Willie T. and me, then they all turned their heads and gazed solemnly at the cabin behind them.

Then, "He up there," Evy said in her soft murmur.

I can't say why, but right then and there something came over me, like a possum had run over my grave, and tears sprang up into my eyes. I don't know if I was just plumb wore out from toiling up the mountain through the weeds and the brambles, or if I was scared by the sad look on Evy's face, but suddenly I was overcome by a wave of grief, and tears ran down my cold cheeks.

I stared toward the little cabin.

"Our teacher?" I gasped.

Then louder, my voice rising to a miserable squeak, "Erskine?"

Witch Boy jumped up and whirled around to look toward the front porch of the little house and he swished his tail a few unsure swipes, then he let loose with a long mournful howl.

The woman at the pot threw her pole down on the ground and grabbed up a handful of wet clothes out of the steaming black pot.

"Take de younguns on up there, Evergreen," she sighed. "Patience, you hep me wrang out de clothes, we hang 'em at de fireplace to dry."

Evy and the other woman named Patience unwrapped their arms from each other, and the three of them made low humming, clucking sounds like brooding hens as they moved about.

"Come on y'all," Evy said as she wrapped her arms around me and Willie T., steering us across the dirt yard toward the cabin and up the high front steps.

Our footsteps, mine and Willie T.'s, were loud as we clattered across the narrow wood porch. Witch Boy's toenails click, click, clicked as he trotted behind us. Evy's bare feet made no sound at all.

As far as I could see, it looked like the house had only one big room. There was a fireplace with a warm crackling fire on the right side of the room, a table and chairs against the back wall, and three low, narrow beds over on the left side. Erskine lay on the nearest bed.

A worse-for-wear rag quilt made out of faded red and brown and green squares covered him up to his chin, and a thin, flat pillow in a white cotton pillowcase was under his head. His face looked too white, way too peaceful for our crazy teacher, and his thick brown hair was combed straight back away from his forehead. His eyes were closed and he wasn't moving. An uncovered window shed pale daylight into the room.

With her arms around us, Evy ushered us up to the side of the bed. My breath came in short choking gasps as I looked at our teacher's colorless, still face.

"Is he dead?" I sobbed. "Is our Erskine dead?"

Evy hesitated and looked at me without saying anything, like maybe she felt sorry for me but didn't want to answer my question. Then she shook her head.

"Not now," she answered softly.

I looked up at her, trying to figure out what in the world she could possibly mean by 'not now,' and I saw that Willie T. looked as puzzled as I felt.

"Not *now*?" he snapped, looking awfully irritated. "What the tarnation does that mean?"

Evy glanced at Willie T. but didn't answer his question.

"That win' blow so hard. I tole 'em, Patience and Safina. Win' blowin' too hard on de mountain . . ." She drew a deep breath, then sighed. "They ain't listen to me. Let it keep on a'blowin'."

We both stared at the girl standing between us. I truly believe that Willie T. caught on to what she was saying way before I did. Or, at least, he thought he caught on.

"What the . . .? You tellin' me it was *them*, somehow made that storm come up?" he yelped, his voice rising to a high screech. Then his voice dropped to a low grumble. "I thought it was the rapture!" I stared at my cousin, totally bumfuzzled. Willie T. can be a trial and a tribulation , but I have to admit that sometimes he does have amazing powers of speculation. "And y'all done it," he added, shaking his head in wonderment.

Evy looked at him, her face as calm as a statue

144

"Now you knows somethin'," she said, then she just barely gave her head one little nod.

We all stood there totally quiet for a little while, pondering. Somewhere outside, the little wren was chirping again. "Secret, secret, secret, secret!"

Evy's arms were still draped around us, and she gave us both a gentle shake, like she wanted our attention. "Now you knows a secret."

The dog put his chin on the pillow close to Erskine's face, and stared intently.

"Lassander," Evy gently crooned. Then she said something, a word I couldn't understand, and the dog's ears went up.

"Why you call him Lassander?" Willie T. asked. "We named him Witch Boy."

Evy leaned closer and looked deep into the boy's eyes. "Don't you 'member this dog? When you jus' a little tike, you had this brown puppy? He be run over, dead in de road! You took him to Studebaker Freeman for healin'. You 'member?"

Willie T.'s face took on a look of amazement. "Stinky Jim?" he said. "That was a long time ago! I had a little brown puppy named Stinky Jim!"

"Studebaker, he brang him all the way up de mountain to us," she continued. "Tote that dead puppy up here in one of he cardboard boxes. He say, 'Too far gone for doctorin'.' Lifted the pore little thang out de box and put it in my hands."

Evy smiled, wrapping one arm around the dog, pulling him into a hug. "Lassander, he know the secret!

"We sent him back down de mountain to you, plenty a' times. He come back ev'ry time, though. Wants to stay up here with us. He gets too big and chase the chickens. Finally, Safina put de spring on he tail. Say she fix him so he forget the way; can't spring back up de bluff!"

The girl clapped her hands and laughed out loud.

Willie T.'s eyes were big as the full moon, his eyebrows raised up nearly to the top of his head.

He patted the dog and wrapped both arms around his neck. "Stinky Jim? This is my puppy, Stinky Jim?" he squeaked, tears filling his eyes. The dog snorted and sneezed, nodding his head up and down like he knew what was going on.

"Stinky Jim!" the girl replied. "I guess he got three names now. Dog with three names!"

Evy started humming the Jacob's Ladder song, soft and low, then Erskine made a low humming sound.

"Look," the girl whispered. "He awake."

"Hmmm?" Erskine hummed again. Then his eyes opened.

*

I heard the two women, Safina and Patience, enter the room, and I turned to see them hanging up wet clothes on a couple of cane bottom chairs in front of the fireplace.

"He awake," Evy repeated, and both the other women slipped quietly up to the bed. Then they all three started clucking and humming again, in some sort of wild up-and-down song. It made the hair on my arms stand up.

The noise they were making seemed to have some kind of effect on Erskine, for better or worse. He raised his head off the pillow and squinted his eyes, focusing on the dog, me, Willie T., then the three women hovering above him.

"The wayward sisters," he sighed. He closed his eyes for just a second, opened them again and looked all around the room and back at the three women, then recited in a dreamy, sleepy-sounding voice.

"The wayward sisters, hand in hand,
three women dressed in strange and wild apparel,
enchanted creatures of the elderwood
brew tempests foul beneath the cherry laurel."

The three women stopped singing and stared down at Erskine Batson, like they were studying a problem. The dog jumped up, bracing his front feet on the bed near Erskine's shoulder, and the room grew still and quiet. Erskine pulled his arms out from under the quilt and raised up on his elbows, smiling and looking dazed but content.

"Mr. Erskine! Are you all right?" Willie T. piped up.

Erskine continued to smile drowsily.

"Fair," he answered. "Fair to middlin', I'd say."

He swept a glance all around the room again.

"So, what sort of mischief are we all up to, now?" he asked, looking a little puzzled.

The woman named Patience heaved a sigh, then stepped away from the bed.

"Up to savin' yo' no count life, is all," she muttered. "Fetch you out from under a fell-down tree, no breff left in yo' no count self," she added.

Erskine continued to smile like a cat that's swallowed a mouse.

"You don't say?" was his cordial response.

"Yes, I say," Patience replied.

Erskine's gaze came to rest on Evy's face, and his drowsy expression changed to wide awake joy.

"Thank the lord! You're okay, then?" he said to her.

"I been okay, the whole time!" she insisted. "It's you was thrashin' up the trail in de mudst of a whirlwind, don't know where you headed, this a'way or that!"

"Runnin' to and fro to destruction!" Patience put in.

Evy laid her hand on the quilt next to Erskine's hand and continued, "You seen me and tuck off you big black coat to wrap it round me from the storm . . . Then the big ole tree come fallin' down, right on top of you! Wham!"

Erskine looked a little incredulous, like he couldn't hardly believe his ears. "I swear," was all he managed to say.

"It all come back to your mem'ry, soon enough," Safina huffed. "Struck on de head, neck broke, breff squeezed outa you. Evergreen, she call to us, to hep get you out from under dat tree. We liff you out, but we let de ole coat stay stuck. Ain't *your* coat, is it? Borrowed or stole?"

Erskine shook his head and answered, "Borrowed."

"I got it, right here!" Willie T. chirped, turning around to show us the black bundle on his back.

"That's how we knew you were lost," I told him. "Brother Goforth found it. Thought it was Principal Vales that was missin', because of the coat. Brother Goforth brought it with him when he came to our house and —"

"And the Chief of Police, too," Willie T. added ominously. "Clyde Tucker."

All three women slowly turned their heads to stare directly at Willie T. like they were starin' at a snake.

"Whoo-ooo! " Safina hooted, a long eerie sound like a ghost on a dark night. That set the other two women off, and they all three swayed and raised a terrible blood-curdling racket, then settled down to milling about, making their busy clucking noises like chickens with their feathers ruffled.

Erskine looked at me and Willie T. and made a puzzled face, mouth turned down and eyebrows up.

"Clyde Tucker cain't come up to de bluff," Safina declared. "That polecat followin' you chilluns up de mountainside?"

"May be," Willie T. allowed. "Him and the preacher, Brother Goforth, was down there at the old stage coach place. And that Ku Klux feller, Olie Hutchins, was with him too."

"I think he's out lookin' for you. Somehow he seemed to be awfully mad about you comin' up here," I informed Erskine, who had begun to thrash around trying to get untangled from the covers. Then he raised the quilt up and stared underneath it with apparent alarm.

"Whoa!" he whooped in surprise., then quickly pulled the covers back up around his chin. "I'm nekkid as a day-old jaybird! Someone has plucked my magic garments from me!"

148

I could tell by his tone of voice that he was quoting from some crazy Shakespeare fol-de-rol.

He looked all around the room. "Where, might I ask, are my clothes? Still under a tree?"

"Was all muddy an' wet," Evy said, shaking her head gloomily. I thought she sounded awfully grieved over the muddy wet clothes.

"Dey be wash and dryin' by th' chimney place," Safina muttered. "Be dry fast enough," she added, and she stomped toward the door, slapping the floor noisily with her bare feet. She glared back at all of us standing around the bed.

"Sister, I ain't lettin' that fool po-lice up here on the bluff, no way," she declared. "Hear me?"

"Hear you," Patience grumbled. Then the two of them hurried out the door and down the narrow wooden steps into the yard.

Meanwhile, Evy grabbed Erskine's clothes from in front of the fireplace, gave them a brisk shake and whispered a few strange sounding words, then placed them, dry as a bone, on the quilt at the foot of the bed. She laughed.

"Is it something else I need to know?" Erskine inquired.

Evy looked just a little bit irritated and shook her head.

"Jus' that Clyde Tucker! He brang papers, say we got to leave this place. Too, he got his eye on Patience! He gwine get his self in trouble with Safina, he keep on."

"Oh . . . so that's it," Erskine grunted. "Thinks I'm sweet on Patience? Which I ain't! I wondered what he'd been jumping on me for, like a duck on a junebug, every time I crossed his path! Blessed me out, said he wanted me to stay away from Moor's Gap! The big muckedy muck!"

"One day he want us all gone . . . Next day he want Patience to stay . . . To an' fro, this a'way an' that! Toil an' trouble."

To say that at this point, Willie T. and I were totally mystified wouldn't have come close to the whole truth of the matter. I was still pondering how quick the wet clothes had got dry. Willie T. was looking all around at the interior of the women's house, lighting his eye first on one peculiar thing then another, meanwhile starin' at Evy like she was Marilyn Monroe or somethin'. And Witch Boy had turned around and around on a little rag rug beside the bed and curled up for a long winter's nap, it looked like.

Out of nowhere, Evy announced, "It gonna snow."

Twenty

The Highwayman's Story

Evy steered Willie T. and me over to the fireplace and we sat on the ancient looking cane bottom chairs, gazing into the dancing fire. The fire sure felt good after being nearly froze to death, tromping around out on the mountain all day. I could have gone sound asleep sitting up, right there in the chair. Willie T. kicked his legs back and forth, tapping the chair rungs with his feet.

"We need to get out of here and head home, you know it?" he whispered nervously. He pulled Erskine's rolled up black coat off his shoulders where he had carried it all day, and began untying and unrolling it. "We need to take Erskine with us and skedaddle. Thangs is gettin' weird."

Evy looked at me, then at Willie T. "Wait a bit," she said in a soft, quiet voice. "I tell you a story."

Erskine made a noise behind us, and I turned around and saw that he had his clothes on and was sittin' on the side of the bed, pulling on his brown leather work boots. When he saw me looking at him, he smiled and said, "I feel a little light headed, yet."

He stood up and ran his hands through his hair, causing it to fall into its normal uncombed arrangement. He stretched his arms over his head, then laughed and said, "Now people'll be sayin', 'Erskine, you act like a tree fell on you!' "

Willie T. twisted around and glared. "Everybody's been sayin' that already!" he chuckled.

Erskine joined us in front of the fireplace and stood behind the chair where Evy was sitting, and you could have knocked me out of my chair with a feather when he leaned over and kissed her on the cheek! It made me think of the way my daddy always kissed my mama, just the same sweet way, whenever she was sitting at the kitchen table. Willie T. cut his eyes at me in a sly way and kicked my ankle, and I closed my mouth.

Erskine dropped his lanky self down and sat on the brick hearth, felt around in his shirt pocket like he was searching for his Lucky Strike cigarettes, then gave up, not finding any.

"So, then! Tell us that story," he said.

Evy drew a slow deep breath, and spread her hands like she was showing us the scene where her story took place.

"It snowed early, that year. Cold moon, high in d' sky, Harvest done come, and de witchin' season about. An' de man come ridin' up in the moonlight, jus' like always. Horse hooves clatterin' on the hard road. Horse named Beauty, and de girl he love named Bessie. Daughter of ol' Solomon Penny, a blackamoor, landlord of th' stage coach stop. Man on de horse a white man, highway robber name' Tom Weaver, come ev'ry night to give his sweetheart a kiss . . . and sometime silver coins and jewels he stole off de stage coach." Evy paused and touched one of the ruby earrings she was wearing.

"Snowflakes be fallin' soft on the mountain, early. This time, when Tom Weaver ride up to de place, militia be waitin' for him for the bounty on his head. Bessie, standin' at the window, see him shot dead on de groun'. Ol' Solomon run out de house, hold up his hands to stop 'em from shootin'. Dey shoot him dead right beside Tom Weaver.

"Militia mens take the body of Tom Weaver away, to get they bounty money from the governor. Leave ol' Solomon Penny there on the ground in th' bloody snow. "

Evy sighed. "Bessie bury him herself, behin' the stage coach stop, an' she carryin' Tom Weaver's baby. Tore de ruby earrings from her ears, thowed 'em on the bloody snow. Leff' the stagecoach stop, move up here to de bluff where nobody dare to touch her, evermore. Talk go aroun', said Bessie a witch. Ev'rybody 'fraid to bother her."

Evy sighed again and sat up straight in her chair, smoothing her skirt with her hands. I felt like a big empty hole had come up, all of a sudden, in my chest.

"Man led the militia, Holbert Tucker. Clyde Tucker's mean ol' great-gran'daddy."

Willie T. and Erskine and I all looked at each other.

"Huh!" Erskine huffed. Willie T. was busy wiping his cheeks on his coat sleeve.

After a while, Evy continued. "Clyde Tucker ain't no *bad* man. But Safina Weaver? No ... she won't forget."

Erskine looked like he was studying the situation. "Well, I'd say that was a long time ago," he said.

"Long time ago," Evy agreed, nodding her head. "But de memory still in de blood."

Erskine and Evy both stood up at the same time.

"Patience, she Safina's little sister. Safina won't turn loose," Evy sighed.

I looked at the pretty girl who stood beside me staring into the crackling fire, and I wondered where she fit into this whole story.

"Are you Safina's sister, too?" I asked.

Evy straightened her skirt, touched her hair, and pulled her long black braid forward, over her shoulder. "Somethin' like that," she answered, but then she cast a warning glance at me and Willie T. "Part of the secret," she cautioned.

Erskine looked puzzled. "What?" he asked, looking from one to the other of us, but Evy just shook her head. Then she opened the front door and looked out.

"Snowin'," she said.

Twenty One

Snow

Willie T. and I rushed to the door to look at the snow, something you don't see too often on Moonlight Ridge. And I've got to say, I'd *never* seen a snow like that one. Huge soft clumps of snowflakes drifting down, looked almost like white feathers falling slowly from the sky.

Evy, still barefooted, and Erskine, now wearing his long black coat, stepped out onto the porch to watch as my cousin and I clambered down the wooden steps and ran out into the yard, holding our hands aloft to catch the drifting snowflakes as they fell.

The crow, Midnight, swooped down from the top of the roof with a loud cry, landing on the ground between us, where he began prancing around like a little soldier, pecking at the snow that had already started covering the yard. Soft white snowflakes dotted his shiny black feathers and gathered on top of his head.

The snowfall got faster and thicker.

Safina and Patience stood by the big black pot, now emptied of its hot soapy water.

"I guess I not be cookin' no chitterlins out here today with this snow," Safina spoke as she used her long stirring pole to scatter clumps of dirt and snow over the dying fire.

"Umm-ummm-umm-umm," Patience hummed, then Safina and Evy took up the tune and they all hummed across the yard in long, mournful sounding tones. Midnight flopped onto his back in the snow, his long hideous feet kicking up and down in what looked to me like a joyful spasm. Willie T. giggled and kicked a blob of snow in the ridiculous crow's direction.

I turned to look at Erskine and Evy standing on the porch, and saw that Erskine had his arm around the girl's shoulders.

Suddenly Witch Boy launched himself out of the cabin door and skidded to a halt on the porch beside Evy's bare feet. The fur on his brown back stood up in a ridge down his spine, and he barked like he intended to eat somebody up. The crow left off rolling on the ground, lifted his enormous wings, and flapped away into the snowy distance.

"Dey here," Safina fumed.

Lo and behold, Police Chief Clyde Tucker thrashed his way out of the bushes, and I was surprised to see Brother Goforth right beside him.

"Now, let's be calm," Brother Goforth said in sort of a hurried, soothing tone. He gripped Clyde Tucker's sleeve and held on. "Let's be calm, now," he repeated.

"Calm, my back foot!" Clyde Tucker growled. "Erskine Batson got no bidness, up here messin' around. I'll take care of his little red wagon!"

Erskine descended the porch steps, followed closely by Evy and the snarling dog, and he walked over to face the huffing and puffing chief of police.

"Officer Tucker," he said in kind of a smart-alecky way. "I understand you have some concerns about my welfare, but as you can see, I'm fit as a fiddle. And no laws are being broken here."

"I can thank of a few," the red-faced policeman grumbled, glancing around at Safina, Patience, and Evy. Snow was falling hard and thick in the yard.

156

Safina pulled her long stirring pole out of the empty black pot and pointed it in the police chief's direction. "You cain't thank of nothin' but some no-count meanness, like the rest of yo' no-count pasty-face fam'ly!" she snapped. I watched Clyde Tucker's pasty face lose its confident expression and change to something closer to indignation.

"Now, that ain't fair!" he whined, running one hand over his face like he might be trying to wipe something off. Then he pointed his big stupid finger right at Safina. "President of the bank wants this place for a huntin' club . . . I done explained it all to you, and you up here holdin' up progress! All I ask is you to sell it at a reas'nable fair price. Move on into town like I tole you . . . I been patient with y'all folks, and you know it! And me, I been patient with Patience . . ." and his voice sort of trailed off.

"Patient with Patience," Willie T. mumbled beside me.

Brother Goforth's hands were raised up in the air like he was either about to pray or surrender, and his eyes were locked on the tall policeman beside him. Clyde Tucker, with snow gathering on his shoulders and piling up on the top of his police cap like meringue on a pie, reared his head up a little taller and glared at Willie T.

"What the blue blazes is these kids doin' up here?" he demanded, as if he'd just now become aware of our existence. I looked to my cousin for an answer.

Not one to reliably stick to the subject at hand, Willie T. squinted his eyes at the falling snow and announced, "What I want to know is, was that really the Possum Man that we saw down there on the side of the mountain, or not? He looked just like the Possum Man, didn't he Lily C.? But Possum Man's been dead this whole long time, and I know it! And if it wadn't Possum Man . . . "

Clyde Tucker gritted his teeth and looked like he couldn't decide whether or not to jump into this discussion, the preacher nodded his head and looked like he was formulating a theory, and the three women all began milling around and making their disturbed chicken noises. Suddenly Safina threw her pole down on the ground, just barely missing the policeman's black boots.

"Snow on de ground!" she announced. "I'm goin' in de house, get me some shoes on! Come on, Patience," she commanded, and tore out across the yard, bare feet crunching on the inch or two of snow covering the ground.

Patience stole a sly look at Clyde Tucker. "Comin'," she grumbled, and followed her stampeding sister across the yard, up the wooden steps, and into the cabin.

Erskine stared at the two men, the tall, rangy policeman, and the nervous looking preacher.

"And, where's your Ku Klux buddy at? I was given to understand that he was taking part in your little excursion today."

"Olie? He got a case of the jitters and I sent him home," Clyde Tucker informed us. "A little ole rabbit run out of the bushes and tried to climb up his pants leg, like to scared him to death. He said he believed it weren't no ordinary rabbit, and he lit out back down the mountain!" The police chief cackled and stomped the ground.

Witch Boy growled.

Erskine Batson, meanwhile, glanced around the yard, scratched his head, and chuckled like he thought the discussion was over.

"I never seen such a snow in my lifetime!" he declared. The shoulders and sleeves of his black coat were just about totally white with snow. "I'm takin' these students home, while we can still navigate. Field trip's over."

"But . . ." Willie T. objected.

Clyde Tucker stuck his hand out toward us, like he intended to keep everybody right where they were.

"Wait just a gall-durned minute!" he snapped. "You ain't in charge here! There's legalities to be considered. And I mean to find out what's goin' on up here in the first place!"

158

Evy swished her skirts and made a threatening noise that sounded like a low rumbling purr, or a growl, and Clyde Tucker jerked his hand back like he'd been bit.

"The thang is . . . " he began, then stopped and stared at Erskine. "For one thang, what are you doin' with 'Fessor Vales's coat?"

"Good lord! Who cares what I'm doin' with 'Fessor Vales' coat!" Erskine exclaimed. "None of your blasted business!" he shouted, then he turned his attention to Evy.

"You need to get back in the house," he told her. "You're barefooted as a haint!"

And we all got quiet and turned our gaze toward Evy. Witch Boy stopped circling and growling, and he cozied up against Evy's legs and sat down, leaning against her skirt. Brother Goforth stepped forward, took a good look at the beautiful girl, all up and down, then placed his hand on her arm like he meant to escort her into the cabin. But when he touched her, everything changed. The air felt different, and somehow I thought I could hear something . . . music . . . coming from the falling snow around us. Brother Goforth stopped and stared straight into the girl's eyes, and she stood perfectly still, calmly gazing right back at him. He stood there, not moving a muscle, and stared into her dark eyes for a long time, like he was looking at something so amazing that he couldn't quit looking.

Finally, his mouth fell open and he made a little noise, something like a soft chuckle, and he held onto her arm a little tighter as he asked, "And you are?"

"Evergreen," she answered. "These folks calls me Evy."

"Evergreen," the preacher repeated, nodding his head like he knew that was right, and tears welled up in his eyes. He turned then and looked at us like he couldn't believe his eyes and ears. Like he suddenly knew something, and wondered if we knew it. Like he suddenly knew a secret.

He nodded toward the cabin, a look of wonderment still on his face. "And those other ladies . . . ?" he asked.

"They sisters," Evy answered. "Safina Weaver and Patience Weaver. Just womens. They owns this place, legal. I be stayin' with them . . . long as I please."

"I'll swear," Brother Goforth replied, staring into Evy's eyes again.

Erskine looked at Evy like this was a revelation to him. "But, I thought . . . " he began.

"What?" Clyde Tucker barked. He glanced around at all the rest of us, like he suspected something was up. "What?" he asked again.

And me? I was just keeping my eyes and ears open, feeling pretty sure that something *was* up. I looked around and saw Safina and Patience standing in the open door of the cabin. And I saw that it had stopped snowing. And just like that, Midnight came sailing out of the woods and landed pretty as you please on Evy's shoulder.

"Lord have mercy!" the young preacher gasped, and I couldn't tell if he was praying in the ordinary way or truly asking for help. He turned loose of Evy's arm and held both hands up in the air again, smiling like he'd never seen a prettier sight in his whole entire life.

Even Clyde Tucker appeared to be at a loss for words.

Willie T. just muttered, "Crazy bird," then scuffed his feet in the snow and shrugged his shoulders. "We gonna stand around here all day passin' the time, or what?" he demanded. "What time is it anyways? I'm hungry!"

Everybody let out a loud breath.

"Right. Right," the preacher said, heaving a sigh. "Now, we'll *all* head on back home. Won't we, Brother Tucker? Ever'thing's fine here, I believe. Wouldn't you say ever'thing's fine here, Brother Tucker?"

Clyde Tucker shook his head and snorted, "Ar'right, preacher. Fine! Fine!" Then he looked disgusted and added, "But we ain't finished here, not by a long shot. It's a bid'ness deal, fair and square."

Brother Goforth turned his attention back to Evy.

"Ma'am, Thanksgivin's just three days away. We'll be havin' a Thanksgivin' service at the church on Thursday night. We'd be honored to have *you* there with us." Then he waved his hand toward Safina and Patience at the cabin door. "All y'all," he added. "We'd be truly blessed."

Erskine smiled, still looking dazed and more than a little puzzled.

But I saw the look on Evy's face.

Twenty Two

Thanksgiving

I came down off the mountain that day, not sure what I had seen or what I'd been told. I knew the words, but somehow it didn't make any sense to me, and I couldn't put it all together in a way that I could understand. All I knew for sure was that, by hook or by crook, our teacher had survived a tree falling on him, and that he showed every sign of being in love with a strange beautiful black girl on Cat Bluff whose name might be Evergreen, and that folks called her Evy. And that she went barefooted in the winter time, wore ruby earrings, and had ugly scars on her ears. And then there was that business about the dead puppy that turned out to be our Witch Boy, as alive as any dog could possibly be.

And I certainly didn't know what to make of the Police Chief, Clyde Tucker, 'having his eye on' Safina's sister, Patience.

Willie T. said it was no mystery to him; he'd seen it all on *Search for Tomorrow* and *The Edge of Night*, the soap operas that Aunt Rachel watched every day on their new RCA Victor television set.

Mama and Daddy didn't know what to think when Willie T. and I both insisted that it snowed up on top of the mountain, and when we told them we'd been all the way up to Cat Bluff, they both dismissed the whole story as a made-up tale.

"Watch out, a painter'll eat you!" Daddy said with a chuckle, and Mama just said "Cat Bluff!" like she didn't even believe it was a real place at all. I guess they felt like they had already dealt with enough strange occurrences: a dust storm and a tornado, a hail storm and the rapture, and that was about all the trouble they could put up with for the time being.

"And them women up there? They might be witches, but they ain't near as scary as comin' face to face with the Possum Man out in the middle of the woods!" Willie T. declared.

Daddy looked shocked and skeptical.

"Pore ol' Possum Man!" he said, shaking his head mournfully. "He's *been* dead and gone, and you know it."

"Willie T. Nock, you make up the awfullest stories I've ever heard!"Mama declared. "You're as bad as Jasper Nash!" And she sent him home for his supper. It was pitch dark outside, and so cold that for once Daddy drove Willie T. home in the pickup truck instead of letting him walk the half-a-mile by foot.

So the way it ended up, Willie T. and I pretty much kept all the secrets to ourselves.

*

Thanksgiving Day came, cold and bright. Mama and Daddy, Granny Rilla, Mawmaw Laurie, Papa Jasper, Aunt Rachel, Uncle Buddy Nock, Henry Hope, me and Willie T. and Witch Boy, all crowded around our kitchen table. Mama, up before daylight, had cooked all morning long, making turkey and dressing, mashed potatoes and gravy, a great big pot of Hoppin' John, Henry Hope's favorite food in the whole world, and a sweet smelling Lane Cake, my daddy's favorite desert. Granny Rilla brought a great big pan of scrumptious persimmon pudding and a plate full of warm, sweet raisin biscuits. Our little kitchen was crowded and cozy, everything smelled right spicy, and everybody was in a holiday mood, talking and laughing over the delicious feast. All Aunt Rachel talked about was how glad she'd be when school started back again, and Uncle Buddy said that he'd heard Professor Vales hadn't been missin' at all, but was just asleep in the back room of his house, sleepin' one off, he said, and his wife just didn't think to look there for him.

"Old Lady Vales heard a noise, finally, and called the police back again and told them she thought it was a burglar in the house!" Uncle Buddy reported with glee.

"Clyde Tucker his self snuck through the house with his pistola in his hand, and found 'Fessor Vales, snorin' away, in the back bedroom! Miz Eudora was so mad, she threatened to shoot him herself!"

Uncle Buddy slapped the table, making the spoons and forks rattle, and we all had a good laugh.

After we had all stuffed ourselves full enough to bust a gusset, we attended Thanksgiving Service at the Moonlight Ridge Baptist Church, and Brother Goforth beamed with delight at the congregation of well fed, happy church goers. I noted that the only black face in the crowd was Studebaker Freeman, who gave me and Willie T. a withering glance when he saw us, and spoke loud enough for everybody to hear when he said he sure enough hoped we were keeping out of trouble, for at least a little while.

Evy and Safina and Patience weren't there.

I saw Erskine, sitting on the front pew with his sister and brother-in-law, Estaleen and Cowboy Howard. Erskine took Baby Junior from his sister, and bounced him up and down as Miz Eudora Vales banged along on the old church piano and we sang "Come, Ye Thankful People, Come."

As the song ended, Brother Goforth stood at the pulpit, looking about as happy as anybody could look, gazing out over the room at all the faces in the crowd. He smiled and said, "I'd like to say just a few words to you all here tonight.

Then I'll let us all get on home to spend a little more time with our loved ones on this chilly evenin'.

"Brothers and sisters, I just recently found out that I don't know everything there is to know in this world. And I'm here to tell you, revelations can come to you when you least expect them. And in ways you don't expect. And even when a revelation comes to you, you still might not understand just what it means."

"Amen to that!" Studebaker Freeman called out from the midst of the congregation. "I know that's right!" And there was a general murmuring of "Amen, Brother," from first one pew and another.

The young preacher nodded. "But you'll know there's greater things in Heaven and Earth . . . and you'll carry that knowledge with you, all the days of your life."

With a shock, I suddenly realized for sure that he was talking about his experience, whatever it was, up on Cat Bluff, when he stood in the snow looking deep into Evy's eyes like he was watching a movie at the picture show. Willie T. looked at me and raised up his eyebrows, like he wondered if the preacher was about to let some kind of cat out of the bag. Up on the front pew, I saw Erskine sit up straighter, and he stopped bouncing the baby up and down.

Brother Goforth opened his Bible and held it in his hands, but didn't look down at the words as he continued. "I'd like to read to y'all from the book of Hebrews, Chapter 13. Here's what it says: 'Keep on loving one another, as brothers and sisters. And be not forgetful to entertain strangers, for thereby some have entertained angels unawares.' "

A hush fell over the entire congregation, and I guess each and every person there was considering that message in their own way.

"I truly believe those words, brothers and sisters," the young preacher said. "I know that it's true. Thereby some have entertained *angels* . . . unawares."

For a little while, nobody moved a muscle, and it seemed like everyone was waiting to see if the preacher had anything else to say about it, but he just stood there, looking like he was thinking things over. I heard a shuffling noise somewhere behind us, and turned to see Safina and Patience, standing together, just inside the door of the church. Erskine quickly handed Baby Junior back to Estaleen, and hurried down the side aisle to join the two women, the wayward sisters, hand in hand, as he had called them, standing at the back of the room.

Brother Goforth closed his Bible and said, "Let's sing 'All Things Bright and Beautiful.' "

Miz Eudora Vales struck up the tune on the piano, and we sang together about all things bright and beautiful, all things wise and wonderful.

All Things Bright and Beautiful

All things bright and beautiful,
all creatures great and small,
all things wise and wonderful,
the Lord God made them all.

Each little flower that opens,
each little bird that sings,
He made their glowing colors,
and made their tiny wings.

The cold wind in the winter,
the pleasant summer sun,
the ripe fruits in the garden:
God made them every one.

God gave us eyes to see them,
and lips that we might tell

how great is God Almighty,
who has made all things well.

All things bright and beautiful,
all creatures great and small,
all things wise and wonderful,
the Lord God made them all.

    As soon as the song ended, Brother Goforth, still clutching his Bible to his chest, left the pulpit and skirted down the side aisle to stand with Erskine, Safina, and Patience. Erskine appeared to be arguing with the women about something, and as Willie T. and I ducked through the crowd, trying to make our way to the back of the church to see what was going on, I saw Erskine waving his arms around over his head, thrashing the air just like he did when he had the breath knocked out of him when we all fell into the hole.

    I noticed right off that Safina and Patience were both wearing shoes: black open-toed high-heels with white bobby socks.

    "You listen to me! You listen to me," Safina was saying, and the preacher patted Erskine on the back like he was trying to comfort a baby with the colic.

    A few people stood around, lingering here and there to say a few parting words to one another, but just about everybody edged around Erskine and the preacher and the women, eager to make their escape from whatever drama was unfolding. Mama and Daddy were talking to each other when they passed by, and Mama just glanced quickly at us then walked on without saying anything.

    "She ain't comin'," Safina said, shaking her head. "Son, she ain't comin' down from de bluff, and you knows it."

    "I'll go find her, then!" Erskine declared.

    "Cain't find her," Safina answered. "Got her own ways. She come and go, like you knows she do."

Patience made one of her soft, clucking hen sounds. "The singin' here is mighty pretty. Fine as I ever heard."

Erskine gazed at the ceiling and turned around like he was searching for help. Safina spoke again before he had a chance to figure out what he wanted to say next.

"You got these childrens to tend to," she said, shaking her fist at me and Willie T. "Not much mo' than a chile, your own self. You stay away from dat ol' place, stay down here where you b'longs, and teach the little childrens at yo' school. And they's other childrens, all over the creation, could sure use your help. Mind the bid'ness at hand, 'cause times is changin', and dey gonna change! You teach these here little ones the right way to grow up, love one another like brothers an' sisters, like de young preacher here say! Dat's yo' work to do!"

Erskine looked from face to face, his mouth falling open like he still couldn't light on just what to say.

"That's right," Brother Goforth agreed, nodding his head. "She's right. We each one have our own little part to do. Things will be different in times to come. It's . . . "

"But what's that got to do with it? What's that got to do with Evy?" Erskine demanded. "I can go back up there and see her!"

Safina shook her head and grabbed ahold of Erskine's sleeve. He was wearing the black coat, and she gripped his sleeve and gave it a shake.

"It ain't for us to say, when we see her an' when we don't. She save you from dat fallin' down tree, and that's that. Now, you got no mo' bidness up there. We got that crazy po-lice to deal with; you got de childrens to teach. De world keep turnin'." Safiina shook her head again and patted his sleeve. "All I gots to say.

"Come on, Patience," she commanded.

"Comin'," Patience answered, rolling her eyes, and the two women turned and left us standing there.

Erskine looked bleak.

"Preacher?" was all he said.

Brother Goforth shook his head. "It's a mystery," he replied. "It's just a mystery."

*

Thanksgiving Holidays came to an end, and we went back to school feeling like the whole world had changed. Willie T. and I stopped digging for artifacts; it got dark too early to do much exploring after the school day was over, and the weather was too cold. Papa Jasper and Mawmaw Laurie said it was the coldest winter they could remember, and they could remember quite a few.

Just once or twice we bundled ourselves up in layers of coats, scarves, gloves, and toboggan caps to wander up Moor's Gap Road, and late one cold, gray afternoon, we saw Erskine, looking miserable and hopeless, sitting on the old stone wall of the stage coach stop. Willie T. looked about as miserable as our teacher, and he said "Come on, Lily C. Let's leave him alone." And so that's what we did.

If he ever saw Evy again that autumn, we never heard anything about it. And I don't believe that he did.

He spent a lot of time in our class room standing silently at the window, staring out into the gray school yard like he might be watching for someone to appear in the distance. But nobody appeared.

Willie T. and I were the only ones in the room who had any idea what was on our teacher's mind, but every one of the students could feel what kind of mood he was in. And so we all just waited.

Professor Vales, black-haired and beady-eyed as ever, stopped by our room pretty often, and talked quietly to Erskine, then winked at all of us and encouraged us all to keep our noses to the grindstone. Then one day Willie T. drew the funniest picture I've ever seen of a pitiful fellow leaning over with his long nose against a huge round grind stone, with sparks flying out in all directions. He gave the picture to

Erskine, and lo and behold, our teacher cracked a smile for the first time in a coon's age!

Then he stuck the drawing on the bulletin board with a thumb tack, laughed out loud, and announced, "Well scholars, it's time we get back to exercising our eyeballs!"

And it was "Pencil! Grindstone! Pencil! Grindstone!" till we were happily wore out with all of our exercised eyeballs.

And me? I wished that I could make sense of what had happened, and wished I knew how much to believe, and how much to try to forget. I thought a lot about what the preacher had said, about entertaining angels unawares. Almost every night I looked out my bedroom window into the black winter sky, halfway expecting to see or hear a big black crow trying to peck his way through the hoarfrost on the glass. But I felt pretty sure that Midnight was one crow who was not exactly an angel, unaware or otherwise.

I didn't know if we'd ever see Evy again. And I never could decide what to think of her . . . or the wayward sisters, for that matter. I just knew that life out on the mountain was a never-ending revelation, and I repeated the preacher's words to myself, over and over.

"It's a mystery. It's just a mystery."

But more than anything else, through those blustery winter days and the silent, frozen winter nights, I thought about the beautiful ruby earrings on the bloody snow, and every time I thought about it, I felt like my heart was breaking all over again. And I believed that the preacher was right when he said, "You'll carry that knowledge with you, all the days of your life." And I remembered the words of the song that Papa Jasper had sung to us, it seemed like such a long, long time ago, conjuring up the ghosts of the highwayman, Tom Weaver, and his beautiful sweetheart, Bessie Penny.

And still, of a winter's night, they say,
when the wind is in the trees
and the moon is a ghostly galleon tossed upon cloudy seas,

when the road is a ribbon of moonlight,
looping the purple moor,
oh, the highwayman comes riding, riding, riding,
yes, the highwayman comes riding, up to the old inn door.

We have always lived with ghosts on Moonlight Ridge.
And now . . . for better or worse . . . witches.

Photograph from the Hugh Mangum Collection
Used with permission from
David M. Rubenstein Rare Book & Manuscript Library
Duke University

Ramey Channell

Glossary

Chitterlings or **chitlins** — an economical dish, usually made from the **small intestines** of a **pig,** although the intestines of **cows** and other animals are sometimes used.

Euclid — An ancient Greek mathematician; the founder of the study of geometry.

Hominy — Hulled corn from which the bran and germ have been removed. The word hominy seems to have arisen from Captain John Smith's 1629 interpretation of the Algonquian word apppuminnee or appuminneonash, meaning parched corn.

Indian summer — A period of unusually mild, warm weather, occurring after a period of colder weather, usually in late October or early November.

Lane Cake — Emma Rylander Lane of Clayton, Alabama, in Barbour County introduced the classic treat bearing her name in her self-published 1898 cookbook, *A Few Good Things to Eat.*

Loup-garou — In **Cajun** legends, the creature is said to prowl the swamps of Louisiana and possibly the fields or forests of the bayou regions. A legendary creature linked to European notions of the werewolf. Sometimes referred to as the rougarou, it is described as a creature or a male witch with a human body and the head of a wolf.

Moor — A member of a Muslim people of North Africa, of mixed Arab and Berber descent, who established a civilization in North Africa and Spain. (756 – 1492)

moor — a tract of wasteland or unenclosed ground

Painter — Colloquial pronunciation of the word 'panther'.

"Pluck my magic garment from me." — Quote from Prospero in *The Tempest,* Act I Scene 2, by William Shakespeare.

Pythagorus — Greek philosopher and mathematician who greatly influenced the development of mathematics and its application to music and astronomy.

"Wayward sisters, hand in hand," — The Three Witches or Weird Sisters or Wayward Sisters are characters in **William Shakespeare** 's play *Macbeth.* The name "weird sisters" is found in most modern editions of *Macbeth.* However, the First Folio's text (1623) reads: The weyward sisters, hand in hand.

RECIPES

Persimmon Pudding

3 cups persimmons
2 cups buttermilk
1 stick plus 1 tablespoon unsalted butter
1 ½ cups unbleached sugar
3 eggs
1 ½ cups unbleached all purpose flour
½ tsp salt
1 tsp baking powder
1 tsp baking soda   1 tsp cinnamon
½ tsp nutmeg   ½ tsp ginger

Preheat oven to 350° F. Grease a 4 x 8 x 12 inch pan with 1 tbsp butter.

Puree 3 cups persimmons, which will yield 2 cups puree. Combine puree with buttermilk. Beat stick of butter and sugar until fluffy. Add eggs one at a time. In a large mixing bowl, stir the puree into the butter/sugar/eggs.

Sift all dry ingredients together and fold them into the persimmon mixture. Fill baking pan with mixture, place the pan into a larger pan and fill the larger pan halfway with warm water.

Bake uncovered for 1 ¼ hours or until the pudding is firm in the center and has pulled away from the sides of the pan, and a knife inserted into the center of the pudding comes out clean.

Serve hot with whipped cream or vanilla ice cream.

How to puree persimmons: Remove skins from ripe persimmons. Persimmons can be mashed through a colander, and seeds will be removed and left in colander. If using a food processor, remove seeds before processing.

Chitterlings (Chitlins)

Fresh or frozen chitterlings
3 or 4 bay leaves
2 stalks celery chopped
2 cloves garlic, minced
1 tbsp whole cloves
Salt and ground red pepper
Beaten eggs
Cracker crumbs

Soak chitterlings in cold water and wash thoroughly. Each chitterling should be examined and cleaned of all foreign matter. Rinse in several changes of cold water. Chitterlings should retain some fat.

Cover with boiling, salted water. Add bay leaves, chopped celery, minced garlic, whole cloves, salt and ground red pepper.

Cover and simmer until tender, or approximately 3 to 4 hours.

Drain and cut into pieces. Dip each piece in beaten egg then in cracker crumbs.
Fry in deep fat or oil until brown.

Ramey Channell

Hoppin' John

½ pound bacon, diced
1 medium onion, chopped
2 stalks celery, chopped
2 cloves garlic
1 tsp chopped parsley
Black-eyed peas, cooked and drained
Salt to taste (1 tsp salt for 2 cups dried black-eyed peas)
Cooked white rice

Sauté diced bacon, chopped onion, and chopped celery until onion and celery look translucent. Drain grease. Add garlic, parsley, and cooked black-eyed peas, simmer until peas are tender but not mushy.

In a large pot or bowl, gently combine peas and cooked rice, or serve peas separately over mounds of cooked rice.

Note: Before cooking dried black-eyed peas, sort through them thoroughly for tiny pebbles or other debris, then rinse and drain.

Note: Cooked ham, chopped, can be used in place of bacon.

Raisin Biscuits

2 ½ cups unbleached self-rising flour
1 egg (optional)
Small pinch of salt
1/3 cup butter
¾ cup milk
1 tbsp unbleached sugar
1 ½ cups raisins

Preheat oven to 450°.

Sift together flour, pinch of salt, sugar. Cut butter into the flour mixture. Beat egg and add to the milk, stir into flour/sugar mixture. Add raisins. Turn onto well floured board, knead gently, using more flour if necessary for a smooth dough. Cut with small biscuit cutter and bake at 450° for approximately 15 minutes.

Ramey Channell

Lane Cake

1 box white cake mix, baked in 2 layers according to directions and cooled completely.

Filling:

8 egg yolks, beaten
1 cup sugar
½ cup butter
1/8 tsp. salt
1 tsp vanilla extract
2 cups pecans chopped
2 cups golden raisins
1 small can crushed pineapple, drained
1 cup grated coconut, optional

Use double boiler to cook first 4 ingredients over boiling water, stirring mixture constantly, until thick.

Remove from heat and add vanilla, pecans, raisins, pineapple, and coconut. Cool slightly.

Split cake layers to form 4 thin layers.*

Alternate layers of cake and filling, finished with a layer of filling on top.

*How to Split Cake Layers Using Thread or Dental Floss

Cake must be completely cool. Use a ruler to locate one-half way up the side of cooled cake layer for placement of toothpicks. Place about 6 or 8 toothpicks inserted into side of cake layer at half-way mark, all the way around. Wrap a long piece of thread or dental floss all the way around cake, using the toothpicks as guide. Cross ends of thread and pull with steady pressure. Thread will pass through cake layer, cutting it evenly into two. Remove toothpicks, and alternate 4 layers of cake with filling.

Ramey Channell

Book Club Discussion
The Witches of Moonlight Ridge

1 - *The Witches of Moonlight Ridge* leaves a lot of questions unanswered. What are some of the topics in the story you feel are left open for speculation?

2- What are some of the unusual circumstances concerning the ruby earrings?

3 – What questions arise concerning Erskine's black coat? Why did he take the coat off in the storm? Who was wearing the coat when the tree fell, and what are some possible explanations for the coat being left under the tree?

4 - What does Clyde Tucker give as his reason for wanting the women to move away from their cabin on Cat Bluff? Why do you think he was angry about Erskine spending time on Moor's Gap Road and at Cat Bluff?

5- How does Evy's story about the Moonlight Ridge highwayman, Tom Weaver, compare to the story in Alfred Noyes' 1906 poem, *The Highwayman*? What are some of the similarities?

6 – How do you feel about Brother Goforth's reaction when he meets Evy?

7 – What symbolism or meaning do you think could be attached to the name Evergreen?

8 – What is the possible connection between Bessie Penny and Evergreen? What do you think Evergreen's relationship is to Safina and Patience? What are some reasons for Safina wanting Erskine to sever his relationship with Evy?

9 – References to witches and ghosts seem to be commonplace on Moonlight Ridge. What are some ways witches are mentioned? Lily Claire says, "We have always lived with ghosts on Moonlight Ridge." What are some examples?

10 – What do you think of Erskine Batson as a teacher? In what ways do you think the children in his classroom received lasting benefits from Erskine's teaching techniques?

About the Author

Growing up in rural Alabama, Ramey Channell was spellbound by family stories of extraordinary beings and peculiar visitors. Her inspiration springs from a world where Alabama backwoods and backyards are visited by numinous creatures, and gardens are filled with echoes of enchanted song and laughter. Ramey's award winning poetry, short stories, and children's stories have been published by Alabama Writer's Conclave, Scholastic Press, Alabama State Poetry Society, River's Edge Publishing, *Aura Literary Arts Review, Birmingham Arts Journal,* and others. This is her second novel in the Moonlight Ridge Series.

CPSIA information can be obtained
at www.ICGtesting.com
Printed in the USA
LVOW07s0254181217
560134LV00040B/2777/P